THE MOCK REVOLT

Also by Vera and Bill Cleaver

I WOULD RATHER BE A TURNIP

THE MIMOSA TREE

GROVER

WHERE THE LILIES BLOOM

LADY ELLEN GRAE

ELLEN GRAE

THE MOCK
REVOLT

Vera and Bill Cleaver

J. B. Lippincott Company   Philadelphia / New York

❧ ❧ CHAPTER ONE

It was a morning in May in the year 1939 and Ussy Mock, thirteen years old, was on his way to get his hair cut. He had orders to go to Arkie's Barber Shop and allow Arkie to thin and shape his pale, wavy crest so that it would lie flat and round and to suffer Arkie to snip his sideburns to just the right length. His parents wanted his head to look like his father's.

Though it was early in the day, just a little past eight o'clock, it was already very hot. The sun was hidden and the air was sticky. To the west of the town gray clots of smoke dotted the sky; there was a brush fire in the hammock. The neighborhood houses of Medina were deathly peaceful and deathly quiet in the 90-degree heat. They were not all the same and the people who lived in them differed from each other in this way and that and yet there was a sameness about them and their inhabitants that always frightened Ussy a little whenever he stopped to think about it. Ussy had a word for the people of Medina; he called them deadlies. He himself was in danger of becoming one and that was the issue this year.

On a downtown corner Ussy met his friend Turner Ensley who was also thirteen years old. Turner lived with his brother (whose nickname was Directly) and was as free as a sparrow. Nobody ever ordered him to school or church or opened his mail or confronted him with a failure. Turner had the most exciting head Ussy had ever seen. It was shaved except for an inch-wide strip of dark red fuzz running north and south from his forehead to the base of his skull. Turner's brother had created this hairdo. It made Turner look like a red-headed Iroquois Indian.

Turner was barefooted and he was bare to the waist; nobody had ever said to him that it was wrong to run around town half bare-naked. He reported eating a dozen raw oysters for his breakfast. "Hot, ain't it," he said and fanned his forehead with his palm.

"Yeah, it's hot," agreed Ussy. "We had fried eggs. Nobody at my house has ever ate a raw oyster except me. For some reason my mother thinks they aren't nice. Look at how I'm dressed, Turner."

"I was looking," said Turner. "But I wasn't going to say anything."

"Even on Saturdays," said Ussy, "I have to get decked out like this. Just because my father is vice-president of the bank."

Turner made no reply; he had heard the complaint a thousand times and had run out of replies. He went with Ussy to Arkie's Barber Shop which was the cleanest, oldest business establishment in Medina and sat in a chair by the window and watched Arkie give Ussy the conventional haircut ordered by Ussy's father.

Arkie thinned the pale crest until the waves lay flat and round. He measured the length of the sideburns with a little ruler and carefully snipped.

"If you could leave my sideburns just a little bushier this time I wouldn't mind it," said Ussy, testing his luck. Arkie's talcum was smothering him. "They itch when you cut 'em so short."

Arkie's hands were firm. His voice was firm. His scissors were cold against Ussy's head. "You don't want bushy sideburns. What for?"

"So I won't look like everybody else in this town."

"You'd look strange," said Arkie, "with bushy sideburns. Do you want to look strange?"

"Yes," admitted Ussy.

Arkie swung the big barber chair around so that it faced the mirrored wall and the marble shelves containing the bottles of shampoos, tonics, and hair conditioners. "I'm not in the business of making people look strange. Your daddy's going to pay me for cutting your hair the way it should be cut so that's what I'm going to do. Sit still, please."

Ussy sat very still and Arkie pushed his head down

to shape the back neckline. Ussy crossed and un-crossed his legs. When Arkie finished with him his head would look exactly like his father's and several other dozen heads in town. Not Turner's though.

Arkie finished the haircut, removed the white neckcloth and apron, reached for a bottle of lemon-colored hair tonic. He upturned the bottle and sprinkled Ussy's head liberally.

"I don't like that stuff on my head," said Ussy. "It stinks."

Arkie massaged and combed and he did this al-most reverently. His breath smelled like Juicy Fruit gum and the sweet-spicy smell of his body talcum was powerful. He moved around to stand in front of Ussy —to admire his artistry.

"Nobody else thinks it stinks. All my other cus-tomers like it. I use about a gallon of it a month."

"I don't care if you use ten gallons of it a month, it still stinks."

Arkie permitted his church-deacon smile a small exercise. He had no qualms at all about any of his judgments. He moved to one of the sinks to wash his hands and Ussy got out of the barber's chair and stood beside it. He looked at himself in the mirror, then across to Turner who was noisily leafing through a magazine and then to the bottle of lemon-colored tonic that had been put back on its shelf. Its color made him think of something. An idle idea came drift-ing across the back planes of his mind.

Arkie was drying his hands on a clean towel. "Think I'll go across the street for a cup of coffee. I'll put the charge for your haircut on your dad's bill. There wasn't anything else you wanted, was there?"

"No," answered Ussy and was careful not to look at the bottle of yellow hair tonic or allow any emotion in his voice. "A guy is supposed to meet Turner and me here. I told him I'd wait here for him. If that's all right with you."

"Sure, sure," said Arkie. He took some change from the cash register, locked it, and started out the door. He came back to say to Turner, "Next time Directly goes snapper fishing tell him I'd like a mess. Ten pounds or so."

"I'll tell him," said Turner.

Arkie left the shop and went across the street to Delphine's Cafe. Turner laid his magazine aside and stood up. He came across the room and walked around Ussy twice, critically appraising his head. "It's weird," he commented. "If you was twenty years older I'd swear you was your father standin' there."

Ussy took the bottle of lemon-colored hair tonic from the marble shelf and held it up to the light. There was a bulge of excitement in his stomach. "Look at this, Turner. What does it make you think of?"

Turner turned and leaned close to the bottle. "Well, I don't want to be vulgar."

"It makes me think of the same thing," said Ussy, stroking the bottle. "Now tell me something; what if we was to do with this bottle what I'm thinking?"

Turner was backing away. His eyes were wide. "No, Uss. No."

"Turner, it wouldn't be anything. It'd be just a

9

little joke on all the deadlies. Actually we'd be doing them all a favor. It'd make their hair shine. I just got through reading a book by a great Yukon explorer and he says that's what Eskimo women use on their hair to make it shine. He comes right out and describes it in his book so it's nothing."

"If it's nothing," argued Turner, "then why are we wasting our time talking about it? Ussy, you want some raw oysters? I saved you a dozen. Directly brought 'em from Appalachicola last night. They're so fresh they're still wiggling. You want 'em or don't you?"

Clutching the bottle, feeling the taste buds in his mouth swell and then drain, Ussy regarded his friend. After a long moment he put the bottle back on its shelf. "That wasn't fair," he said.

Turner let Ussy walk out the door of Arkie's Barber Shop ahead of him. The two went down the street and stood in front of the Strand Theater gawking at the glossy billboard pictures of Dimple Dewey who was starring in the current attraction. Turner remarked that he just didn't think too much of Dimple. "She just ain't too swift," he said. "She ought to close her mouth and hide some of those teeth. It's just not natural for her to hang her mouth open like that. It's just not natural for her hair to be that color either. Directly took me to see this picture and I can tell you right now it just ain't any too swift. There's a place in it where Dimple is supposed to be asleep and her boyfriend who's a sheik comes tiptoeing into her tent. He's just come from fighting a bunch of Arabs in the

10

desert. One of them has just stabbed him in the side and another one has clobbered him in the head—he's got a rag tied around it. He's got blood all over him and there's a knife sticking out of his back but all he wants to do is get to Dimple Dewey so he can kiss her and ask her to marry him. The Arabs are coming after him. They're screaming outside Dimple Dewey's tent. One of them has got thrown from his horse and another horse has run over him. They're making enough racket to raise the dead but Dimple Dewey is just laying there asleep with her mouth hanging open. This is one of the funniest picture shows I ever saw, Ussy. You seen it yet?"

"No," answered Ussy. "My parents won't let me. They say it's dirty."

The sun had come out of its hiding place. Now it was high over the town of Medina and the clots of smoke from the brush fire in the outlying hammock had gone, leaving the sky clean.

Tired of the pictures of Dimple Dewey, Ussy and Turner went across Medina's main street and sauntered southward. They were on their way to Turner's house which was a big, antebellum structure within walking distance of the town but still aloof from it. It had been willed to Turner and Directly by grandparents, both now buried in Arkansas, and was set behind rusty gates and broken walls. The wanton vegetation surrounding it grew to its doors and up its walls and this land was wild and private. Turner and his brother reveled in its spooky loneliness.

In the estimation of Ussy Mock, Directly Ensley

appeared a powerful force. He was untainted by and uncaring for the things which concerned most men. He didn't belong to the Fraternal Order of Eagles, The Elks or any church. He was his own barber. He didn't own a briefcase or a hat and his only tie hung in his closet along with his black laying-away suit. When he felt like it he drank liquor. He owned a motorcycle which, when opened up, could do over a hundred miles an hour.

It was Directly's view that marriage was a snare invented by lazy women and that all children under the age of five were unsanitary. He took good care of his body which was six feet, four inches tall and weighed two hundred pounds naked. He wasn't ashamed of his nakedness the way Ussy's father was. He didn't own a pair of pajamas or a bathrobe. His chest was covered with a beautiful growth of silky red hair and underneath this there was tattooed a magnificent British battleship, H.M.S. *Dreadnought* which had four propellers driven by Parsons turbines, displaced 21,845 tons fully loaded, made twenty-one knots, had ten twelve-inch 45-caliber guns mounted in five turrets, three on the centerline. Since Directly had spent a large part of his life in the United States Navy it seemed odd to Ussy that he would have selected a British battleship for his chest picture, but Directly had a ready explanation for this: "I just wanted to be different," he said.

On this day Directly was cleaning house. He had moved everything movable—chairs, tables, bedsprings, mattresses, dressers, a love seat, and whatnots—from the lower rooms to the yard, had soaped down all the walls and floors and windows with a mop, had hooked up fifty feet of hose to the water spigot just outside the front door. Now he was preparing to rinse. He was barefooted and naked from the waist up and he was disgruntled with the responsibilities of home ownership. "This here is woman's work," he lamented. "I swear if it wasn't so much trouble I'd get married. The day I got discharged from the Navy I swore I had done all the swabbing and scrubbing I was gonna do but here I am at it again, tooth and nail. I swear I never saw so much dirt. Where does it all come from? A man ain't nothing but a slave to it, that's what. Where y'all been?"

"Town," answered Turner and slid his feet back and forth on the soapy floor. "Ussy had to get his hair cut."

Directly's feet were water-shriveled. He had the end of the empty hose in his hand. He waggled it and looked at Ussy. "If you was twenty years older I'd swear you was your father; you look just like him. One of you go out and turn the water on for me; I'm gonna hose this place down. Watch how you move around in here. A soapy deck ain't anything to mess around with. I knew a guy in the Navy who killed himself on a soapy deck. We was down in the Panama Canal Zone when it happened. They gave him a medal for dyin' for his country. His wife tried to sue the Government for two million dollars but that's all she got—just the medal and a little pension. I knew another guy who fell down a manhole and killed himself. That was in San Francisco. They gave him a medal, too. Me, I never got a medal for anything."

"You're still alive," observed Turner.

"Praise be to God," said Directly. "One of you go outside and turn the water on for me and the other one grab that broom over there. There's another one out back in the shed. Shake a leg now; I wanna get through with this sometime today. I got more important things to do."

Within the hour the whole lower half of the house had been hosed down and the water swept out. The outside heat had entered it and the walls and floors steamed. Directly said the wet cleanliness did something good to his soul. He filled three glasses with chipped ice and ginger ale and invited Turner and Ussy to join him for a little veranda refreshment. Turner served Ussy the promised raw oysters. They went down so fast Ussy almost didn't taste them.

The three friends sat on the vine-shaded veranda and drank their drinks and listened to the prolonged, wailing yowl of the limpkins echoing from the surrounding woods. Directly was morose. "I should've been born a bird. One of them limpkins. I got good intentions toward life but just seems like they never work out."

"Well, it's summer," said Turner, trying one of his irrelevancies.

Directly fished a piece of ice from his glass and thoughtfully bathed H.M.S. *Dreadnought.* The silken red hair covering the tattoo turned dark and stood up in little wet points. After a minute he said, "There's a thing about owning a house."

"What?" asked Turner. "What thing?"

With a shrewd air Directly explained his meaning. "It's a responsibility. There's always something needing to be done. It's like a job. Worse maybe. At least when you've got a job and want to quit you can just say so and leave. But not a house. A house is something like being married. You wake up in the morning and there it is staring at you. You go to bed at night and there it is staring at you even after the lights have been turned out. You lay in bed and you listen to the roaches running and the termites chewing and you try to think of ways to get rid of the pesky things before they just chaw up the whole place but everything that comes to your mind costs money. That's why I say there's a thing about owning a house. It's worse than being married or trying to hold down a regular job."

"Next time you go snapper fishing, Arkie wants ten or fifteen pounds," said Turner.

"I don't know if I'm ever gonna go snapper fishing again," said Directly. "It's too much work. It's just too blamed much for what little I get out of it."

"I had a job once," said Ussy. "It was summer before last. Before you and Turner came to Medina."

"A job?" Turner said. "You never told me that."

"I know it. I don't tell many people about it because it was . . . well, it was something a deadly would do. My father got it for me. It was in Davis's Jewelry Store. Did you know that the lever escapement for watches was invented by a guy named Thomas Mudge in 1765?"

"I don't even know what a lever escapement is," said Directly. "I don't think I wanta know either. I got enough stuff in my brain now without adding stuff like that to it."

"Well, it was just a job," said Ussy. "My father got it for me. I wasn't crazy about it. Old Davis used to holler at me when I'd sweep while he was trying to repair his watches. People would come in and stand around and wait for him to fix their watches. The ones that brought in the cheapest ones were the worst about that. They were afraid old Davis was going to steal the jewels out of their clunkers. Which was pretty dumb because the jewels that go in watches aren't worth anything. They aren't real jewels. They're made out of synthetic rubies and sapphires and you can buy a whole bushel of them for around three dollars and jewelers just can't be bothered prying them out of people's watches. It's a lot of trouble to pry them out. And even more trouble to put something else in."

"That's real interesting," said Directly. "But somehow it just don't interest me much. I think we'd better start moving the furniture back into the house. Then I'm going to take me a nice bath and take me a little ride. I know somebody who might be interested in buying this place. I'm tired bein' a slave to it. Maybe I'll just sell it and Turner and me'll take off for San Francisco or somewhere."

Something painful and unsteady went through Ussy. It made his pulse lag and then quicken. He put his hand to his mouth and bit the knuckles. "You would leave Medina? But, Directly, you said . . . I thought you said you liked it here. You said you like all this peace and quiet. And this old house. I know the

16

tucked in the frame of her dresser mirror. They had cost a dime each. Ussy hated Priscilla Lang and was contemptuous of Skinny-Winnie. She was such a deadly. So bossy. So female. She took violin lessons and was always feeding Pody, the youngest member of the Mock family, the wrong answers.

Thinking about Skinny-Winnie, Ussy wished, for the ten-thousandth time in his life, not to be related to her. And he wished, oh, how he wished, Directly wouldn't talk of selling out and moving to San Francisco.

Directly sold his house that day. Toward dusk he came back from town with the news that prospective buyers were coming. They arrived ten minutes later and after an hour or so of dickering bought the house and everything in it. They gave Directly an earnest-money deposit check and agreed to meet him at an attorney's office on Monday to close the deal.

After they had gone Directly pranced around through the house kissing the check and waving it. "Did you see them? They looked like a couple of old down-and-outers, didn't they? Which goes to show you that looks don't mean a thing. They're going to pay me cash! Boy, you just don't realize how unusual it is for somebody to have cash these days! I'll bet they've had it buried in tin cans in their back yard. Boy! I can't believe it! San Francisco, here we come!"

Directly got pleasantly drunk that night. He sat on the darkened veranda with his bottle and Turner close by and sang Navy songs and he and Turner swapped jokes and made plans.

people aren't much; they're all a bunch of c
But you don't associate with them. You wouldr
Medina, would you? Sure enough now?"

The expression on Directly's long, shag
was lightly melancholic. He had cocked his l
one side in an attitude of listening and the limp
the hammock were yowling again—long, wailin
sounding from the cattails and the rushes. Dire
placed one hand on H.M.S. *Dreadnought,* was
its inked outline with a thumb. He said, "Yeah
I think I would. I get to thinkin' about things. I
thinkin' about San Francisco—how it looks wh
fog comes rollin' in from the Pacific. The hills.
town. The Golden Gate Bridge. I just got t
Turner out there and show him all that before
too old and lazy to want to. You know what I
Uss?"

"Sure," replied Ussy and he wanted to go
and pick a fight with his sister Winifred who was
wise known as Skinny-Winnie. She was twelve
old, weighed a hundred and fifty pounds and wa
sionately devoted to radio programs. There wa
she always rushed straight home from school I
was named *Priscilla Lang, M.D.* Priscilla had a
voice and the answer to every problem. She an
patients fought life every day from four to four fi
P.M. and in between the snatches of agonizing
dramatizing the announcer sold facial soap gu
teed to make honeymoons out of even the most ri
marriages. Skinny-Winnie had sent away for g
photographs of Dr. Priscilla Lang. She kept t

After a while of listening to this, Ussy interrupted to ask a favor. "Directly," he said. "I want you to do me a favor. I want you to fix my head up to look like Turner's."

Directly had had just enough to drink. He took his razor and clippers to Ussy's head and when he had finished with it, it was bald except for one pale ribbon of hair running from the forehead to the base of the scalp. It had a center tuft.

❧ ❧ CHAPTER TWO

None of the members of his family saw his head until Sunday morning. He rose very early and scuttled to his Sunday bath with an old shirt draped around his head. There were soft, fluttering snores coming from the room his parents shared and loud, grunty ones coming from Winnie's. Winnie always slept flat on her back with her mouth open. During her sleep she snorted like a horse. She fought her sheets and pillows all night long and in the mornings rose from her bed exhausted.

The door to Pody's room was open. In his pajamas he was sitting at his little play table drawing crayon pictures. All the walls of his room were decorated with hideous faces with misshapen mouths, floating eyes disconnected from the faces, balloons attached to thick sticks, an alarmed-looking brown cow sliding down a purple hill. Pody, six years old, had ferocious artistic ability. Ussy thought Pody was smart. He could write his name, despised *Priscilla Lang, M.D.* on the radio, was entranced with Ussy's stories about Stony Flint, one of Ussy's favorite book characters. Pody and Ussy were friends of a sort. Pody made up his own expressions and nothing surprised him.

Ussy stopped at the door to Pody's room and stuck his head inside. He pulled the shirt from it and pointed to it. "Hey," he whispered. "Look what I got."

Pody looked up and his eyes grew wide. A smile crept across his face. "Oh, it's pretty," he whispered.

"You like it? Really?"

"It's pretty," whispered Pody. "They'll be mad when they see it. Is it Sunday, Ussy?"

With a finger to his lips, Ussy nodded.

"I knew it was," whispered Pody. "The newspaper's bigger. I brought it in." He bent again to his drawings. Absorbed in them, he puffed his cheeks and drew his eyebrows together. He made decisive black strokes and spoke softly to himself: "Aha, she cried as she cracked her wooden leg." The sound of this meaningless expression of his pleased him and he said it again, "Aha, ha, ha, she cried as she cracked her wooden leg."

Ussy went to the bathroom, locked the door, and

21

examined afresh his image in the mirror. Baldly glistening, his head was not so gorgeous as Turner's. It was too pale. The hair stripe with the tuft in its center blended in too much with the naked, cream-colored skin. Still, it was a decided improvement. He looked a little bit evil this way. Reckless. That was the word for his changed appearance.

Ussy summoned a scathing grin to his lips and a sardonic look to his eyes. He swaggered back and forth between the tub and the sink, jutting his snake hips to one side with each step, letting his hands hang loose at his sides. This was the way Stony Flint walked, easy on the balls of his feet, all of him lithe and wary. Stony never carried a gun. The muscles in his arms were like steel bands. Stony was the best roundup man in the entire west, sought after by ranch owners from Alaska to Texas but he preferred the free, unfettered life of the prairie. He scorned money. He and his horse slept every night under the stars, far away from civilization. He was a lonesome loner.

In a gesture acquired from Stony Flint, Ussy hitched the pants of his pajamas and returned to the mirror. When they saw his head there would be a fight. He grinned at himself evilly.

He stayed in his room until he smelled the Sunday bacon and pancakes. Then he sallied forth.

His mother said not a word when she saw his head and his father rose slowly from the breakfast table, syrup pitcher in hand. His father said, "Oh, now. Now what's this?"

His mother was letting a pancake burn. Ussy said,

"Ma, you're letting a pancake burn." He went around his father and sat down. Everybody was looking at him.

"Aha, she cried as she cracked her wooden leg," murmured Pody and reverently dribbled milk on his oatmeal.

His mother was scraping the burned pancake from the griddle. She wasn't going to say a word.

"You look ridiculous!" exclaimed Winnie. "Just ridiculous! You needn't think you're going to church with us looking like that!" There was butter on her chin and she wasn't aware of it. She was rapidly blinking her exhausted eyes and twisting her napkin. In a minute her gathered lament burst from her. "Motherrrrrrr! Aren't you going to say anything?"

"Oh, be quiet," said Mr. Mock. "Shut that up. The neighbors will think we're killing you."

"I don't care!" squalled Winnie. "Look at him! Look at his head! He doesn't look human! And he's related to us!"

"Yesterday," said Pody, stirring his oatmeal, "Winnie didn't do her violin lesson so now for three days she can't listen to *Priscilla Lang, M.D.* I'm glad. I hate Priscilla Lang."

"I look as human as anybody else around here," said Ussy. "What's the agony? It's my head."

"Your head," said Mr. Mock.

"Pop, you're dripping syrup on your pants—"

"What's the big idea, Ussy? Just what's the big idea?"

23

"Pop, there's no big idea. I just wanted my head to look like this, that's all."

"Did Arkie do that to you?"

"No, Pop."

"Who did?"

Ussy bit his knuckles. "I did."

"You couldn't have. You're lying."

"Okay, I'm lying. I'm a liar. But I did it."

"Why?"

"Because I want to look different. I don't want to look like everybody else in this burg."

"Why not?"

"Pop," said Ussy. "You know why not. I've told you before."

"I just don't," said his father, "understand you. I realize that's my fault, of course. I'm old and old-fashioned. I've forgotten my own youth, it's been so long ago."

"Aw, Pop."

His father sat down. He put the syrup pitcher in its saucer. "There is something wrong when a young, respectable man from a nice respectable family wants to go around looking like a lunatic. What is it, I wonder?"

Ussy could not take his eyes from his father. The collar of his father's seersucker robe was turned up high around his neck and buttoned. His hair was brushed; he looked dignified. He looked like a banker except that he wore no jewelry. That would be remedied in another ten or fifteen years. When he would be given a gold watch with his name inscribed on the back of it for twenty-five years of faithful service to the Medina State Bank. Then he'd sit behind a bigger desk at the bank and make bigger decisions. He'd get to be Sunday school superintendent and be on the school board. The Mocks would move to Medina Heights, a newly developing section of Medina, and on Sunday afternoons people would drive slowly by and gawk at their fancy new house.

Ussy repressed a shudder. He loved his father. Why then, couldn't he admire him and want to be like him?

His father was saying, "When I was your age I was out on my own. I had to give up school and go out and work. I had to help support my parents. Nobody indulged me the way your mother and I indulge you. Maybe that's the trouble. Maybe we make everything too easy for you. Do you think that might be it?"

"I don't know," replied Ussy who longed to overthrow the obstacles of ease: food, clothes, spending money, his collection of Stony Flint books, his own clean room with its soft mattress, and pictures of flowers on the wall. What was wrong with him not to appreciate all these good, easy things? A lot of other kids didn't have them. Turner's best jacket was one of Directly's that had been cut down to fit him and he only owned one pair of shoes. Turner walked to and from school and brushed his teeth with Arm and Hammer baking soda. He had pocket money only when Directly had a surplus of it which wasn't often. He slept in his underwear.

It's because I don't want everything made easy for

me, thought Ussy. I want to go out and battle the world. Whammo! Sock it on its jaw! Make it wobble! Whammo! I just got to do it before I get so old I won't want to. If I'm not careful somebody's going to slip me the twenty-five-year watch. I have got to get away from all these arrangements. Go see the Golden Gate Bridge in San Francisco before I get so old and lazy I won't want to. I could join the Navy. If I got me a tattoo first like Directly's they'd think I was older and take me. I could go to the Panama Canal Zone.

His mother was standing over him coldly wanting to know how many pancakes he could eat.

"Just four," he said. "Please."

They all went off to Sunday school and church without him. He was required to wash the breakfast dishes and run the sweeper and it annoyed him that his conscience would not allow him to accomplish these chores sloppily, like Skinny-Winnie.

Finished with the housework he sat in his room reading Stony Flint books but was unable to concentrate on The Loner's adventures. After a while, with a little thrust of regret, he pulled all of the books in this series from their shelf and carried them to Pody's room. He stacked them in a pile and shoved them into a deep corner of Pody's closet, covering them with an old sweater. In a few years Pody would appreciate Stony fully.

He went to the front of the house and stood in the doorway looking out through the screen. The scene in front of the Mock home touched nothing but impatience and boredom in him. The street was hot and

26

silent and the houses had a closed-for-Sunday look about them. Only the gray-green Spanish moss in the trees moved, sluggishly waving with each push of the hot, sluggish wind.

This day would surely bore him to death. There would be the deadly Sunday dinner and then the Sunday ride in the family Packard. Then he'd be forced to accompany his family to the Strand Theater and watch a movie with tap dancing and singing in it.

The movie didn't have any tap dancing or singing in it. The heroine's name was Charlotte and she had huge, tormented eyes and a fatal illness and Skinny-Winnie, sitting next to Ussy, cried. He laughed and offered her his big handkerchief and his father leaned to whisper, "Ussy, if you don't like the movie you can go home."

Ussy rose and squeezed past his sister to the aisle. He went to the lobby and loitered there walking around looking at the pictures of coming attractions. He approached the usher and inquired if Directly and Turner were inside the theater. The usher shook his head. He left the theater and went down the street walking like himself and not Stony Flint. He was through with imitating Stony Flint and there was a certain justice in this. The sky over Medina was the color of a ripe tangerine.

The reflection of his own true image in the windows of the stores did not satisfy. Even the changed appearance of his head which made him think of a cream-colored gumdrop did not now satisfy. He wanted to be with his friends, Directly and Turner. He wanted to sit on their veranda with them and drink ginger ale and listen to Directly's spiels about the places he'd been and the things he'd seen.

Ussy lifted his feet and began to lightly jog down the hot, sun-filled street. The hammock surrounding the Ensley house would be cool. Directly and Turner would offer him iced ginger ale. If he hung around long enough Directly might even ask him to stay for supper.

Directly and Turner were not home. Alone and feeling a little sorry for himself, Ussy sat on their veranda and waited for them to return but they did not. He went inside and aimlessly prowled through the rooms. With a pang he noticed Directly's black laying-away suit and his one necktie had been taken from the closet. An open valise containing Directly's clothes stood on the chest at the foot of the bed. Turner's things, packed in a pasteboard box, stood beside the valise. The valise and the box would be all they would take from the house. Tomorrow or the next day the valise and the box would be tied on the back end of Directly's motorcycle, Directly would hand the key to the house over to the old couple who had bought it, then he and Turner would go out and climb on the motorcycle and roar away to San Francisco. It would be awful without them.

Standing between the box and the valise Ussy felt the true, terrible finality of his impending loss fully for the first time. Without Turner and Directly to provide balance and liberation when things at home piled up on him he would lose his strength. He would be sucked into the machinery of DEADLINESS and after it got through chewing him up and molding him he wouldn't even resemble his present self. He'd be sweet and obedient. He'd look like everybody else and think like them. When he got to be eighteen or so his father would get him a teller's job in the Medina State Bank. He'd work there until he was fifty at which time he would be presented with a gold watch with his name engraved on the back of it, only by that time he wouldn't be able to see it without a magnifying glass because he'd be half blind with age.

Caught up in the uneasiness of this thinking Ussy went back to the veranda and sat waiting for Directly and Turner. He sat on the steps with his head in his hands staring out across the hammock. Where the sun did not penetrate, it was the ugly brown color of swamp water. From the black, peaty floor of it there rose the smell of decomposing vegetation and from the tall, distant trees of it there came the sad, wild calls of marsh birds.

Ussy bit his knuckles and tried to think of a way to cheer himself and after a moment an idea came to him. He left the steps and went back inside the house. He went to the pantry just off the kitchen and located Directly's bottle of whiskey. At the sink he let the water from the tap run until it was cool. He sat at the porcelain-topped table with the glass of water and the bottle of whiskey before him. He held the bottle to the light; the amber-colored liquid in it would comfort and warm him.

Ussy got drunk. Afterward he could remember

little spotted parts of this experience: the way his legs slid away from him sideways when, after the third drink, he tried to stand. The way his brain softened and slithered around in his head, sloshing and gurgling. How the whiskey jolted through his veins. The taste of it in his mouth and along the inroads of his tonsils was sour; it burned. He looked around the room and at first every object in it was startlingly clear. His thoughts were the clearest ones ever conceived. They all concerned his escape from Medina—how he would accomplish that. He would hitchhike a ride to Pensacola. With a truck driver. There he would get himself a tattoo like Directly's. Bigger than Directly's. It would be of a ship on the high seas doing battle with an enemy ship. There would be some mean-looking sharks swimming around it. Gray, with rows of murderous-looking teeth.

Picturing how the tattoo would look on his chest, Ussy grinned and stood up. It seemed important to get to the outside door. He fastened his eyes on it and started toward it. It moved. He set his feet down and stood quite still and so did the door. Casually he looked away from it and then quickly looked again. It was still stationary. He lifted his legs and started toward it again and it moved. He stared at it and put his knuckles to his mouth. "What?" he whispered. "What?" The wind was at one of the windows pushing a tree branch back and forth across its upper pane. *Swaaaaack, swaaaaack.*

Crashing around the room trying to locate the door which moved every time he did, Ussy finally gave up the foolish quest and staggered back to the table. He hung his head and stared at his knees. The door had triumphed over him. It wasn't going to let him leave. A disquieting word came hobbling across the roadways of his mind—ineffectual. He was ineffectual, that's what he was. There was some kind of a failing in him that just wouldn't allow victory even over the smallest thing. He had no effect on people either; they had to be backed into corners and made to listen to his opinions. Then they ran away unchanged.

Ussy stared at his knees and became raptly interested in the cloth that covered them. It was dark blue with a little green thread running through it. Somebody had gone to a lot of trouble to make it. Who? And where? Funny he had never wondered about cloth before. It was a part of his everyday life—of everybody's. Without it people would have to go around naked yet nobody ever stopped to wonder about who made it and where. It was one of the injustices of the world.

Ussy sat in his chair and concentrated on the simple motion of crossing his legs. They didn't feel like they belonged to him any more. They refused to stay crossed. He tried lifting his right thigh with his hands and placing it by force on the top of his left thigh but the leg fell away from him. He gazed at it with distress. Nothing like this had ever happened to him before. There had been times in his life when he hadn't been able to control his brain but he had always been able to command his limbs to lift and move and start and go when he wanted them to. Suspiciously, spying on them, he pressed his thighs and knees together and silently commanded them to stay that way but they fell apart. His eyes filled with tears and at the same time his lower jaw was suddenly and violently pulled downward with a constriction which took sudden place in his throat. His mouth hung wide, an upheavel in his stomach took place and a stream of golden liquid shot from between his teeth.

Before he fell to the floor unconscious, Ussy took the grim, disgusted, befuddled vow never to touch another drop of liquor as long as he lived.

It was nearly dark when he woke and he was still alone. There was pain in the dome of his head and in both temples. His saliva glands had stopped working —his mouth and throat were furry and tinder-dry. He opened his eyes slowly and waited for things to adjust. He lay very still for several minutes listening to the slow, thick cadence of his heartbeats. With each thud a wave of nausea rolled over him. His eyes burned— it took effort to hold them open. He practiced focusing them, first on the dusky ceiling and then on the under-regions of the sink. The paint behind the rusty pipe trappings on the sink had peeled away from the wall, was hanging in loose, little chips. Probably, thought Ussy, Directly's termites and roaches had caused that. I should go home, he thought.

He lay perfectly and delicately still. The dusk on the ceiling deepened and the silence surrounding the house was profound but soon it was broken by the gutteral gruntings of alligator frogs and the hootings of owls. He dozed and became cramped lying there on the hard floor and woke again. The room was astir with warm, heavy shadow; the solitude of the house pushed against him. He cleaned up the mess he had made; he washed himself in Directly's bathroom. He forced himself to leave.

He went home to face his family. He could not explain to them his actions of that day. "But I wasn't anywhere," he protested. "I was just out to Turner and Directly's. They weren't there so I waited for them. They didn't come and I went to sleep. I don't see what everybody's so excited about."

His mother came toward him, sniffing. "You smell."

He backed away from her. "I couldn't."

She came after him, sniffing. "You do. You smell and I know what it is. You've been drinking, haven't you?"

He couldn't lie about it. He was never going to be a drinker. The experience just past had taught him that. He met his mother's look and that of his father's. "Yes," he answered. "While I was out at Turner and Directly's waiting for them to come I drank some of Directly's whiskey."

"Oh, Ussy," said his mother.

He hurried to explain. "It's the worst stuff I ever tasted. I wonder why people drink it. I only had three slugs of it and then I didn't know what I was doing. I can just barely remember. I fell down. I tried to stand up but my legs went sideways, out like this, see? And my head rolled around like this, see? And I couldn't find the door and my brain got soft. Sticky and oozy like jelly. Things were funny. I felt terrible. I feel terrible now. I'm never going to touch another drop of liquor as long as I live."

They began to lecture him on all the things wrong with him; his grades at school and the way he argued with his teachers. The way he questioned the motives of all adults. His choice of friends. And now this—drinking.

"But I told you I was never going to touch another drop," he said. "I got the cure today." His eyes felt red and drawn. He blinked them and tried to look healthy and energetic. "And tomorrow I'll start making better grades at school; I know they're pretty awful. Directly and Turner are going away," he said. "They're going to San Francisco."

They didn't say they were sorry for they were not; they were glad. He could see them thinking how glad they were. He could feel their relief. They asked him if he was hungry. He said no. He said, "As soon as school lets out I think I'll get me a job."

They said they wouldn't object to his having a little job. They asked him if he wanted to listen to the radio with them in the living room. He smothered his scorn for their favorite Sunday night program—*One Man's Family,* so dull and aimless.

When they had gone he went to the bathroom and gulped water until his stomach would hold no more. He brushed his teeth and took a bath. He trotted back to his room and put on his pajamas and bathrobe. His mother and father and Skinny-Winnie were enjoying

34

popcorn and *One Man's Family* in the living room. Pody was in his room, seated at his little work table, drawing a picture of a man feeding a flock of chickens. All of the chickens were colored a violent, waxen red and the man standing over them distributing grain had two right arms.

"Your man looks kind of funny," remarked Ussy prowling around the work table. "He's got two right arms."

Pody gave the man a black cauliflower ear. "I know it."

"He'd look better if you gave him one left one and one right one."

"I know it."

"Then why don't you?"

Pody looked sage and secretive. His chubby little hand hovered over his box of crayons. He selected a brown one and gave his chicken feeder a hat with a drooping brim. "I don't like everybody I draw to look right. Real people don't. I can see things about people other people can't see because I'm an artist."

Ussy drew a chair to the work table and sat down across from his little brother. It was true; Pody didn't see things and people as other people saw them. He saw the imperfections in them. Pody had a little camera in his brain and he went about snapping pictures with it. After these had been developed he transferred them on to paper with his crayons and sometimes the results were causes for alarm. Pody could draw sweet pictures too, though. Ussy was sure he would be a famous artist someday. Right at this moment his potentials for becoming one were being evaluated at a big, Midwestern mail-order school that dealt in art courses. Two forms inviting the enrollment of any interested parties had come uninvited to the Mock house. One had been carefully filled out for Pody and returned. If the mail-order house accepted Pody as a student the art course would cost the Mocks many dollars but it would be a worthwhile investment.

In years not so bygone Ussy had had experience with mail-order houses. He thought they had cheated him at least half a dozen times. The fur on his genuine buffalo-skin chaps and vest was pasted on the skin, his rattlesnake head which should have arrived in a bottle of preservative liquid had been shipped to him in a dry jar, his lifesize ghost guaranteed to float and dart and dance did not float and dart and dance. The most it would do was feebly flutter; it refused to rise more than two feet from the floor. He had written to the manufacturer about it twice but his letters had been ignored. There had been other cases of similar fraud. He knew about mail-order houses. All they wanted was your money. Ussy thought they were a bunch of phony baloneys.

Pody was creating a frame for his picture. He was saying, "If you wanted to, you could find out if you could be an artist. All you have to do is fill out one of those papers they sent. They sent two and Mama only used one for me."

Still suffering from his hangover, feeling hollow and bored, Ussy said, "Where? Where's the other paper they sent? Let me see it."

The form asked how long he had been interested in art.

He had never been interested in art but in the space provided he wrote his meticulous answer: *Six months.*

How old are you, asked the form.

Answer: *72.*

Please tell us what kind of art you are interested in, requested the form.

Answer: *Anything arty. I like to draw pictures of clothes, flowers, trees, birds, little children, babies, fruit, cars, boats, dogs, water, rocks, clouds, the sun, the moon, the stars, Herbert Hoover, Al Capone, and Prince Albert. And so forth.*

The mail-order art school wanted to know the names of Ussy's favorite artists.

He didn't know the names of any artists but in the proper space he wrote: *John Speronis, Allie Athanasaw, Sean Pappas, Semian Jaskas. And so forth.*

Why, inquired the form, would you like to become an artist?

Answer: *For fame and money. And so forth.*

The people at the art school wanted to know how Ussy had learned about their existence and without thinking he gave his answer: *My brother, Pody Mock, told me about it.*

Ussy signed an alias to the form—Casper Bismuth Nestley—and furnished a fictitious address: 323 Avenue of Beauty. He folded the form, slid it into its envelope and licked the flap. "It'll drive 'em crazy," he commented.

He felt better. Carrying the letter which he would

drop in a mailbox on the way to school the next morning, he trotted back to his room and applied himself to the reading of *Silas Marner* by George Eliot. George Eliot had been a woman born with the name of Mary Ann Evans. She was born in 1819 and now, if she were still alive, she would be 120 years old. It was unthinkable to Ussy that her story, in these modern times, could still be considered a piece of classic literature. It was no wonder to him that she had hidden behind a man's name. Her yarn about Silas Marner, a weaver whose lost gold was replaced by a strayed child, disgusted him vastly. It was silly and unreal and had not one thing to do with him or anything with which he was connected.

American history now was another matter. It was a subject that stirred him to the point of fervor. It had taken a lot of stuff for Thomas Jefferson, Patrick Henry, George Washington, and all those other guys to wrest the country from their opposers and set up a new, free nation. Abe Lincoln's Gettysburg address was the greatest piece of poetic literature ever written. Mr. Suffrin, Ussy's history teacher, shared Ussy's devotion to Mr. Lincoln. Also he cautiously shared Ussy's opinion that the citizens of Medina were all a bunch of deadlies who sat on their thumbs watching the world go by.

Mr. Suffrin was not a popular man in the Medina school system or among the citizens of the town. He encouraged his students to have and express their own opinions and much of the time his classroom was in an uproar. He was old—close to retirement age according to Ussy's father. He never attended football games and lived alone in a rented house on a shabby back street. He brought his lunch to school in a tin box and ate it at his desk. In Ussy's opinion, Mr. Suffrin was odd but he was a sweet old guy. He made the learning of history pleasant. There was something about him that produced a feeling of peace.

Ussy put his textbooks away, turned out his light and went to bed. His dreams were serene.

❧ ❧ CHAPTER THREE

It was mid-June and now Turner and Directly had been gone for over a month. They had not kept their promise to write.

School had let out for the summer months and Ussy's hair had made considerable headway in its return to original, correct proportions. Radio's *Priscilla Lang, M.D.* had been replaced with another doctor-program equally as nauseous and a group of Medina's citizens, headed by Mr. Snyder, the president of the Medina State Bank, had caused Medina's Summer Work Camp for Boys to be formed. The purpose of this project was to provide occupation to the youthful, male citizenry. It would keep them off the streets and out of mischief. It would teach them what it meant to be usefully and gainfully employed. They would be chaperoned and supervised. Via a truck they would be transported from their homes each morning to a truck-farming community lying just west of Medina. They would harvest the vegetables grown there. Peppers and green beans, squash, radishes, lettuce, eggplant, tomatoes, okra. They would eat in a dining hall set up especially for them. They would have a thirty-minute rest period in the morning and a thirty-minute rest period in the afternoon. At the end of the workday they would be returned to their homes via the transport truck. The outdoor work would be healthful; there were no dangers involved. At the end of each day the boys would be paid for their labors.

For lack of anything more interesting and profitable, Ussy had allowed himself to be recruited. He was anxious to be busy, tired of being a loafer. He had three days to wait until he could become busy. There was nothing to do but sit on the porch and read the newspaper and try to keep his ears closed to the radio which Skinny-Winnie always kept turned up high. Jar-flies in the wisteria vine beside the porch steps buzzed. In his paper Ussy read that the mayor of Medina was vacationing with his family at a place named Martha's Vineyard. Ussy thought he was a silly, pompous little man. He wore a diamond ring on one of his little fingers and called everybody cowboy.

Ussy sighed, folded his newspaper into a square

and laid it aside. He left the porch and went down into the yard and aimlessly walked around. He was lonely. He should scout around and find out the names of some of the boys who would be going with him every day to the work camp. He needed to make some new friends. It wasn't good for a guy to be such a loner.

He had a dollar and a quarter in his pocket. It had taken some self-control to save this amount; he hadn't tasted a candy bar or an ice-cream soda in over a month. In three more days he'd be a working man. He owed himself a little fling before his nose was set to the grindstone.

Ussy ran back up on the porch and yelled through the screen door. "I'm going downtown in case anybody in there wants to know or can hear me!"

Only the radio howled a reply.

"I might be gone three or four hours!" screamed Ussy. "In case anybody in there cares!"

"I love you," wept the radio.

"Aw, zounds," muttered Ussy.

He went to town and stood idly on a street corner. A soft-drink truck pulled up in front of Delphine's Cafe and inspiration flashed through Ussy. He ran across the street and after three minutes of conversation with the driver of the truck he had a ride to Pensacola.

The driver of this truck was not interested in Ussy, the purpose of Ussy's trip, Ussy's forthcoming participation in Medina's Summer Work Camp for Boys' program, or the German maniac, Adolph Hitler.

Ussy felt compelled to entertain his benefactor.

As they clinked along down the highway toward Pensacola he said, "Must be fun driving a truck like this here. Being your own boss."

"I'm not my own boss," said the driver.

Ussy sat forward in his part of the seat. He knew exactly what he was going to Pensacola for. It was his secret and this was his day. The sun was dazzling on the white, concrete road. He thought he could smell the sea. There was a wad of excitement in his throat. He tried again with the driver of the truck. "Monday I'm gonna start to work. Picking vegetables on a farm. I joined a work camp for boys and that's what all of us are going to be doing. Picking vegetables. Starting Monday."

Ussy's companion was watching his speedometer. There was a passenger car ahead of them and they went around it, the crated bottles on the back clinking. Ussy did not attempt further conversation. In Pensacola he was discharged on one of the main thoroughfares.

He knew what he was looking for and he found it —a long, unventilated arcade containing an array of entertainment devices: Pinball machines, a glass-bellied jukebox. A tattered sign in the lower window corner of this parlor said *TATTOOS*.

Ussy entered this place and immediately the orange paper curtains, that made private a room in the rear of it, parted and a frail old man appeared. He made Ussy think of what the Big Depression was doing to people. He was dirty and hungry-looking. He had very yellow skin. Ussy walked toward him. "It says on the window that you give tattoos."

In a birdlike attitude of attention the sad old man leaned forward. He didn't move from his position in front of the orange curtains. His smile was tranquilizing. "Yes."

"Like to get myself one. I had in mind a battleship. Painted on my chest. I'd like it with a lot of guns. And some sharks swimming around it. How long would that take and how much would it cost?"

The old man considered him. "Tattoos aren't painted on. The skin has to be pierced with a needle."

"Pierced?"

In the bottom of the old watered eyes something faintly proud and contemptuous shone. "The ink that's used in tattooing is indelible; it isn't something that can be washed off. A tattoo marks a person for life. You don't want one."

Anxiety jetted through Ussy's veins. If the old man couldn't be persuaded to give him one he might just as well eternally and completely give up; might just as well concede to everything—all the deadlies. When he had lived his dull life long enough the trumpet would blow for him and he'd be laid to peaceful rest in a graveyard and people would only remember him as somebody who had learned and obeyed all the rules.

The old man standing before the orange paper curtains was watching him. He doesn't like me, thought Ussy. Somehow he knows what kind of life I'm from and he hates me for it. I should go and try to find

44

another place. There might not be one. If when you get a tattoo, your skin has to be pierced that'd hurt. The old man might like to hurt me. He probably doesn't like people who work in banks. But if I don't get my tattoo today I'll never get it.

Painstakingly and, in spite of himself, a little desperately, Ussy began to explain to the old man how things were with him. "My father works in a bank and he teaches Sunday school and he's got a Packard that he never drives over twenty miles an hour and I'm thirteen years old and the furthest I've been away from Medina is here. Last month I got my hair cut different and my parents almost died. My English teacher at school had to read *Silas Marner* when she was thirteen years old so now *I* have to read *Silas Marner*. In my whole life I've only had two friends and my parents didn't like them because they didn't look like other people or think like other people. They've gone away now. When I get to be eighteen my father will probably get me a job in his bank and I'll have to work until I'm fifty. I'll bet you didn't have to read *Silas Marner* when you were thirteen and go to work in any bank when you were eighteen. I have just *got* to get myself a tattoo. Don't you see why?"

Ussy got his tattoo, two hearts beautifully outlined in blue, shot through with a connecting red arrow emblazoned on his right thigh. This site was chosen because it was the safest; nobody ever looked at his bare thighs. It was his seal of independence, his very own, not to be shown to anyone until the right time came. Within the hearts, forever to be a part of him, there were two words—GOOD LUCK.

"Sorry about the battleship," said the old man, remarkably steady as the electric needle in his hand went in and out, forcing ink, drawing blood, hurting. It was torture. Ussy kept his teeth and his hands clenched and at one point in this operation felt his face whiten dangerously. And there was the disappointment about the battleship. The old man didn't have a pattern for one and Ussy's skinny expanse couldn't have accommodated anything so large anyway.

"This will get sore," predicted the old man. "It will fester and scabs will form. Don't pick them off. Just let them fall off naturally."

"Yes," said Ussy through his teeth. He couldn't look any more at what was being done to him. "And remember," said the old, crafty one. "It's a secret where you got this. It's just between you and me. I don't want anybody coming around here causing me any trouble. That was the deal."

"Deal," said Ussy. The tattoo had cost him a dollar and he didn't know how he was going to get back to Medina.

The old man's grin was devilish. "With me it was a fellow named Andrew Lang, a Scottish man of letters. My mother had the romantic notion that if I could be made to share her love of poetry and fairy tales the temptations of the world would pass me by. So I read such stuff as Lang's *Ballads and Lyrics of Old France, Grass of Parnassus,* and *The Gold of Fairnilee.* None of it prepared me for my later life. I was sixteen before I had my first original idea. I stowed away on a ship bound

46

for Singapore and I can tell you right now the temptations of the world went with me every foot of the way. Not knowing what they were I could hardly wait to get my hands on them. It was pretty strong stuff for a kid like me. I almost didn't make it out of there alive. Not knowing anything about life I was pretty curious about it and one day looked at the wrong thing and got myself knifed. I almost bled to death before the police found me."

It was over. Ussy had his tattoo. The old man accompanied him as far as the street door. "Luck," he said, grinning.

"Luck," replied Ussy. He limped down the street to a corner and stood there for quite a while feeling sick. It was long past noon and his stomach was empty. In spite of the precautions he and the old man had taken there were ink and blood stains on his right trouser leg. He'd have to try and think up some logical story to explain these. He had only twenty-five cents in his pocket and he was miles from home. He might not be able to hitch a ride back to Medina, but he had to try and this deserted corner wasn't the place to do it. The main highway running out of the town was several miles over.

Ussy started across the street. He spoke softly to himself. "Aha, she cried as she cracked her wooden leg." His leg hurt. He laughed aloud.

✤ ✤ CHAPTER FOUR

It was Monday, the day the Medina Summer Work Camp for Boys became functional. It was six A.M. and Ussy sat on his front porch reading the morning paper and waiting for the transport truck. His tattooed leg was still sore but the pain furnished an odd kind of pleasure. The tattoo was nicely encrusted now with a shiny brown garland of little scabs; he could hardly wait for them to fall off.

He heard the transport truck coming; it was in the next block over, backfiring, making a turn in someone's driveway. Dogs barked. Ussy left his paper on the porch and went down and stood at the curb.

The dented, thickset truck came around the corner of his block. The driver was going slowly, looking at house numbers. Ussy's mother had come to the Mocks' front door. Her hair was in curlers and she had her robe wrapped around her. She called to him. "Ussy, did you eat breakfast? Why didn't you call me? Ussy, don't go off without any breakfast now, you hear me?"

"I ate!" he screamed. The truck was pulling in at the curb. The open back end of it contained an assortment of boys, some grinning, some solemn. One of the grinning ones offered a hand. He went up into the truck and was pushed toward the cab of it. "Everybody sit down!" bawled the driver of the truck.

Ussy sat down beside one of the gloomy ones. The wind ruffled his growing hair. The air rushing past was cool and smelled good. He felt queerly neutralized. It was a sense of freedom that lifted him. He was on his way to work. He would earn money. He would hoard it and when there was enough of it he would go to Pensacola and buy a motorcycle. He would get on the motorcycle and head west; to New Orleans, to Houston, to San Francisco. He would find Turner and Directly. He would see the Golden Gate Bridge. He would never come back to Medina.

Ussy wanted vastly to tell someone—anyone—about his tattoo for it was this that set him apart from the other boys in the truck. He knew a couple of them; Sammy Hicks whose father owned Medina's haberdashery and Donnie Crowder. Donnie didn't have a father. His mother sewed for people. Ussy disliked Sammy whose specialty was dirty jokes.

The motion of the truck was jostling its live cargo. It was out of the town now and on the rough, graveled road leading west to the truck farm. The boys sat in straggled groupings. Some of them were trying to talk above the noise the truck was making.

The gloomy one sitting next to Ussy with his back against the cab was unknown to him. He was dark and tacky and sullen. He was aloof and contemptuous and this was no pose; it was real. Without a reason he reminded Ussy of Turner and Directly.

Ussy put his hand over his tattoo. He rubbed the palm of it lightly over the cloth that covered it. He leaned toward the gloomy one. "I'm Ussy Mock."

The boy did not draw back or lean forward. "So what." It wasn't a question.

"So I thought you might like to know. We're gonna be working together and eating in the same place every day so it's just natural for me to tell you my name and for you to tell me yours."

"Who says so?"

"I do. Hey, this is some ride, huh? I'll bet we're doing fifty. He oughta take it easy going through some . . . of . . . these . . . holes. Zounds. There . . . must . . . be . . . a million holes in this road and he's hitting . . . every . . . one. What's he . . . mad at?"

The gloomy one's answer was deliberately cynical. He turned his head and looked at Ussy squarely. "Ask me something that ain't so hard to answer. He's mad at himself. Me. Everybody. He stays mad. He's my dad."

50

Looking into the bold bitterness of the dark eyes which held his, Ussy moved his hand away from his tattoo, tucking it into his belt. He couldn't, after all, share his secret with this person. There was something not right with him.

The truck went around a curve sharply and some of the other boys were thrown against each other. Sammy Hicks said a vulgar word and beat his heels against the floor bed of the truck. Everybody but Ussy and the boy sitting next to him laughed. They were on smooth road now; there were no holes.

Ussy pushed his back up tight against the truck's cab and bit his knuckles. He didn't want the boy sitting next to him to explain why his dad was mad at every-body. He had his own problems pretty much under control now. He had plans. He was going to work hard and avoid trouble. For the others this project wasn't going to be a thing in the world but one big horse-around. That much was already making itself known.

Then the boy began to impart indifferent infor-mation about himself. "We live on this farm where we're going. We work there. We had to get up a hour early to go after you."

"Sorry," said Ussy. He wasn't sorry at all. He just wanted the truck to reach the farm so he could get out of it and away from this bellyacher.

"The pump was broke so we didn't even have water to make coffee. It's always broke. My mother's sick. My dad got a doctor to her last night. He says it's malaria. She had it before we came here. Last year when we were out in Colorado workin' sugar beets she had it bad."

A little stab of distress went through Ussy. He was sitting next to a migrant worker—one of that vast horde of homeless people who followed the crops. He knew about them from the newspapers and the once-a-week newsreel that always preceded the movie at the Strand Theater. They traveled by whatever means they could lay their hands on; usually by old broken-down trucks with a dozen kids hanging on the back and all their old broken-down possessions packed helter-skelter. Streams of these workers poured into Florida every year but there was usually nothing around Medina for them. The big produce belts were farther south.

Ussy began to inch away from his companion of the moment. He didn't want to hear about the mother with malaria and all the other troubles. Now he didn't even want to know the bellyacher's name.

"I'll tell you my name," said the bellyacher. "It's Luke Wilder."

"Pleased to meet you," muttered Ussy. The truck was turning, leaving the highway, going up a narrow dirt lane.

Ussy rose and so did Luke. They stood together with their hands on the side slats of the truck railings. Up ahead was a big white house and beyond that there were the truck gardens, acres of them, shining bright green in the early sun. "I don't live in that house," said Luke. "That's where the owner lives. At dinnertime I'll show you where I live. It's way back out of sight over there. We're gonna get separated now in a minute but at dinnertime I'll come to where you'll be eatin' and I'll find you and I'll take you back and show you where I live. I wonder could you do me a favor."

Ussy turned his head to look at Luke. "What favor?"

Luke's return look was steady. "When you have your dinner take a extra piece of meat for me. Wrap it up in something. I'll get it from you when I come for you. After you finish eating. There won't be much time but there'll be enough for me to show you where I live. It's real interesting; you can tell your friends about it."

Something strange and helpless caught at Ussy. This kid looked poorer than potato peelings. The poor ones liked to make you feel guilty, these Depression victims, like it was your fault your dad had a job and you didn't have to stand in line for the free government soup at school. The soup wasn't bad—thick with chunks of meat, vegetables, and oatmeal or rice. Actually it was a better lunch than you could take from home. A five-cent bowl of it would fill your stomach. Ussy always paid but there were those who couldn't. Like this boy with the mad father.

He didn't want to do any favors for Luke. He didn't want to see where Luke lived—the poorness and the sick mother. Already he disliked Luke. But there was this strange, helpless feeling. He floundered in it. "All right; I don't mind. But why can't you eat with the rest of us? I don't see . . . well, why are you asking me to bring you a piece of meat?"

Across the thin, sallow face there went a look of tender craftiness. "You don't understand. I *work* here. The rest of you have just come to play. I won't be allowed to eat with the rest of you. They've already told me I couldn't. But I'll come to where you're going to eat after you've finished. You won't forget, will you?"

He couldn't say no. He bit his knuckles. "No, I won't forget." How would he smuggle a piece of meat out of the dining hall? What would he wrap it in? It would make a grease stain in his pocket.

"We're going to be friends," said Luke.

"Friends," said Ussy. He didn't want to feel anything toward Luke. He tried to push the strange, help-less, guilty feeling away but it was with him to stay.

✍ ✍ CHAPTER FIVE

The members of the Medina Summer Work Camp for Boys had been oriented. They had been shown where they would eat—in a long, breeze-through room with filmy green curtains and clean, bare tables. And where they would rest. This area was in one end of a long, barrackslike building with canvas cots, coolers of drinking water, and a little first-aid station. This last was a card table containing rolls of adhesive tape, gauze, salves, headache remedies, a bottle of iodine and a bottle of rubbing alcohol.

They had met their supervisor, Packy Snyder,

who was a nephew to the president of the Medina State Bank. Packy was a college student, home for the summer. He had a brown, stiff crew cut and a prominent Adam's apple. He had small, close-set blue eyes and called the boys from Medina "men." "Now, men, let us understand each other. We are all here by common consent. Right?"

"Right."

"In the interests of a common cause. Right?"

"Right."

Packy's shoes looked like the same kind Ussy's father always wore—Florsheims with wing tips. Ussy knew they were expensive. They were always displayed in the window of Hicks' Haberdashery. All the businessmen in Medina wore them; so far as Ussy knew they only came in one color—brown.

In his shiny, brown Florsheim shoes Packy Snyder rocked back and forth. He was commanding the attention of the boys gathered around him. "Men, let us clearly understand each other. Do any one of you have the slightest animosity toward his being here?"

"No."

"Do you know what animosity means?"

"No."

"If you don't know what words mean you shouldn't just arbitrarily agree with them. Animosity means resentment. All right, so now that's understood. It is understood that no one has any resentment toward his being here. Right?"

"Right."

"All right, that much is understood. Now we come

to the rules. We have to have rules. Agreed?"

"Agreed."

"And we have to adhere to the rules. Right?"

"Right."

"Do you know what adhere means?"

"No."

Packy's Adam's apple escaped from his shirt collar. He shot his cuffs. He put the tips of his fingers to his temples and pressed. "But I just got through telling you that when you didn't understand things you weren't just to arbitrarily agree. Oh, well, it isn't that important. The important thing is that we're all here and we're ready to start our project. Our project is to go out into the fields and harvest the vegetables growing there. We will be systematic and orderly about it. We will file out of this building in a soldierly manner and go to our work. I am going to assign each of you his own work area. There will be no overlapping areas. There will be plenty of work for everyone. To work, that is what we are here for. I regard you as little men and you will be treated as such. There will be no fighting and no bickering. You will not spit on each other or hit each other. You will just work. If any of you has a legitimate complaint you will come to me. Understood?"

"Understood."

"I am your supervisor. I am here to direct your efforts. I will not stand for any nonsense. I will not tolerate any insubordination. Understood?"

"Understood."

"We will go now," said Packy, "to the fields."

In a soldierly manner they trooped to the fields and the hot sun shining down on them grew hotter; the coolness of the morning disappeared. They knelt in the black earth and pulled and cut the tender, growing things. Packy walked up and down between the rows, supervising the labor. "Men, leave the dirt in the ground where it belongs. Well, shake as much as you can off. We're not interested in the dirt here; we're interested in what the dirt has produced. You see these crates? Why do you think they were placed here? They are to hold the vegetables. When you have filled them properly they will be taken to the wash-shed. There the vegetables will be washed and made ready for market. What is your name, Son?"

Ussy looked up at Packy. "It's Ussy Mock."

Packy's brown shoes had become coated with black dirt. He had put on a pair of sunglasses and the lenses of these were filmed over with dirt and the steam from his sweat. Packy did not grin like a man; he smiled like a woman. Yet behind this meager, limber exercise there was something lusty and a little mean.

"Son," said Packy, "I am to be addressed as sir."

He meant it; it wasn't any joke. The vegetables were pulled and cut; the crates at the end of the rows were filled and Luke Wilder and his father came after them in the thickset truck and Packy Snyder was "sir."

"Sir, I feel a little bit sick to my stomach."

"Sir, my legs are killin' me."

"Sir, I'm choking to death. I know I'm not supposed to eat any of this dirt but I can't help it. I've gained five pounds since I've been out here."

"Sir, if I die between now and quitting time you'll let my mother know, won't you? She'd worry if I didn't come home when I'm supposed to."

"Sir, I hate to bother you again with another senseless question but when are we gonna eat? My stomach thinks my throat's been cut."

"Sir, did we have our rest period? We must have because that's one of the rules but I can't seem to remember it."

Packy was a good straw boss. The gripings and groanings of his underlings affected him not at all. He listened to them and smiled his mean, limber smile. After a while he carried an empty crate to a shady spot beneath a tree and sat there until noon. Then he took a whistle from his pocket, put it to his lips, blew it, and announced that it was chow time. In a soldierly manner the members of the Medina Summer Work Camp for Boys filed back across the green fields to the mess hall. They washed themselves at an outside pump and went in the hall and the food was already there before them, big bowls of it steaming on the tables.

Packy sat at the head of the table nearest the window. He had been the first at the pump but had missed some of his dirt; around his hairline there were black water scallops. He had rolled his shirt sleeves up and loosened his collar. Steam from the hot food rose from the bowls to the ceiling; the room was stifling.

This was the dinner hour but still there were rules. Damp from their pump dunkings, dirty, hot, and hungry, the boys were scrambling for seats. They were wrangling and punching and pushing. They were snarling and yelling.

With his spoon Packy rapped on his plate. "Attention! Attention!" He stood up. "Men, you will seat yourselves quietly. *Quietly!* This is a dining room not a gymnasium. Sit down. *Sit down,* I said, and shut up!"

The boys found seats and sat down. They glared at Packy and Packy seemed not to care that they were hating him. Tenderly and sadly he smiled at them. He sat down, spread his paper napkin, and picked up his fork. He lifted a forkful of vegetable to his mouth. Now he wasn't looking at anything in particular; he was just absorbed in his food.

Ussy was helping himself to a portion of meat from the platter on his table. It was roasted the way he liked it and there was a boat of brown gravy and a bowl of white, boiled potatoes. He was remembering his promise to Luke Wilder—to take him a piece of the dinner meat. How would he manage it? Wrap it in his napkin, of course, and then tuck the little package in his shirt front. When Luke came for him he would give him the meat but he wouldn't go with him to his house. He would make up some excuse not to go; say he was too tired, which was the truth. He was dog tired. He had filled more crates than anybody on his row. There was only an hour before Packy would blow his whistle to go back to the fields. Packy was a first-class dimwit—a real boob. College wasn't teaching him much; it wasn't teaching him how to treat people. It was correct to call your elders "sir" but Packy didn't deserve to be called by that title. He wasn't a "sir." He didn't even know how to talk to people more ignorant than himself. All he knew how to do was strut around and give orders. Packy had an ugly, bully streak in him.

The other boys at Ussy's table weren't talking; they were just eating. There was low conversation down at the far end of the room. Packy had made his point.

Ussy squeezed lemon juice into his glass of iced tea, added six heaping spoons of sugar, stirred and lifted the glass to his mouth. He stopped, fascinated. Traveling high and fast a potato went past his eyes. It reached the wall just beyond Packy's head and fastened itself there, a pale, glistening button. Gravy from it dribbled down. Packy jerked around to stare at it. Another potato came. This one caught Packy at the base of his skull and broke. It slid down Packy's collar.

Packy jumped up and whirled. "Who did that? Come on now! Stand up, whoever did that!"

No one moved. No one spoke. No one stood up. The room was very quiet. The green curtains at the windows did not stir and the little rivulets of gravy on the wall in back of Packy slid downward.

Packy did not repeat his demand. His Adam's apple appeared to swell and his eyes were darting this way and that and up and down the length of the room, speculating, but he said nothing more. With his handkerchief he cleaned the potato from the back of his neck. In a minute he seated himself again; he spread his napkin over his lap and took a sip of his tea. The boys at the far end of the room lifted their forks; they began to talk to each other as if nothing had happened.

Ussy tasted his meat. It was a little too salty but good. He opened a biscuit and ladled gravy over it. A tacky shadow made a noise at the screened door; it was Luke Wilder come for him.

Ussy speared two hunks of meat from the platter on his table and wrapped them in his napkin. He slid the little package inside his shirt and held his hand over it. This business with Luke was sour grapes. Why had he let himself be talked into it? He wasn't anybody's keeper. His table companions were watching him. One of them was objecting to the meat theft. "Hey, you're not supposed to do that! The rule says you're not supposed to take anything from the table. You're supposed to eat it here."

Ussy made no reply. Safeguarding the meat in his shirt, he slid from his chair and went to the door. He opened it and stepped outside and joined Luke.

Luke was a pain in the whatzis. It was embarrassing to watch him wolf the meat. The boys walked a few yards away from the dining-hall building and while Luke ate the meat, Ussy tried to reason his way out of going to the Wilder house. "I didn't even have my own dinner. You didn't give me time. I'd better go on back. Packy didn't say anything about me coming out here but everybody else is eating and that's what I'm supposed to be doing. It's one of the rules; we're supposed to be eating now. I'd better go on back now."

Luke had finished eating. He had swallowed both pieces of meat in four bites. He wiped his greasy fingers on his trousers. "But you said you wanted to see where I lived. That's why I'm here. To take you so you can see."

"Luke, I only said it because I . . . well, isn't it just a house? You can tell me about it. Tomorrow. I've got to go back now and eat my own dinner. There are only a few more minutes left. Packy only gives us an hour to eat."

Crestfallen, eyes stained with disappointment, Luke stepped back. "Don't you want to see where I live? I told my mother about you. She's waiting. She's sick; I told you that."

"Luke, I got to go back and eat my own dinner. There just isn't time today—"

"Yes, there is. There's plenty of time. You got thirty minutes. Look here. I got a watch. I borrowed it because I knew you'd be worried about the time. Look here; it's only twelve thirty. It'll only take us ten minutes to go to my house. You've got plenty of time. My mother's expecting you. I told her about you. You wouldn't want to hurt her feelings, would you? I told you she was sick."

"I know you did. I don't want to hurt your mother's feelings but don't you understand? I've got to go back and eat my dinner now. I haven't got time for anything but that now. I had to work like a dog this morning and I got to work like a dog this afternoon. I don't see why it's so important for me to go look at your house—"

"Oh," said Luke, "you're just like all the rest—"

"What rest? Who?"

Luke's eyes were blazing and his mouth was bitterly curled. "You're just like everybody else. They make promises but then they don't keep them. I should've known. It's my fault. I shouldn't have told my mother you'd come."

"I'm *not* like everybody else," said Ussy. "Don't say I am again." They were wasting time and now it was beginning to seem a little foolish not just to give in and go. It wouldn't hurt him to skip a meal; his stomach would survive. He'd eat some raw vegetables. They'd give him strength. This whole business with Luke—first the meat and now the trip to look at the house and the sick mother—was a pain in the whatzis. The best thing to do was go on and get it over with and be through with it.

The strange, helpless feeling he had experienced earlier—the one concerning Luke—was with him again. He looked at Luke. "All right. I'll go see your mother and look at your house. We'll have to hurry though. Which way is it?"

Luke's good humor was immediately restored. As the two went down a narrow, sand road and then through a harsh, uncultivated region to the house of the migrant Wilders Luke didn't stop talking. "We're only gonna be here till the cold weather. Then we'll go on down farther south. That's why we haven't bothered much with fixing up this house we're living in. You sure live in a nice one."

"Yeah," said Ussy.

"I saw your mother. She's pretty."

"She looks okay."

"What does your dad do?"

"He works in a bank."

"A bank? Really?"

"I didn't say he owned it," said Ussy and was surprised at the sharpness in his voice. "I just said he worked in it."

Luke looked at the sky. "Packy owns part of this place. Did you know that? His uncle gave it to him."

"Good for Packy," said Ussy.

"I got four brothers and three sisters. I didn't tell you that, did I? But I'm the only one living at home now. Marsh, he's the one next to me, got himself adopted out in Colorado. The rest of 'em went on down to California to work. They'll make out okay. Day before yesterday I went with my dad and Packy and we got a bunch of cows. Two bulls, too. That's what Packy studies in college. Husbandry, he calls it. And he studies how to grow vegetables. I think Packy's smart. What do you think about him?"

"Oh, I like him," replied Ussy. His feet and the backs of his knees ached. "Where's your house? Aren't we about there?"

Luke grinned and pointed and the dingy little house was there just up ahead of them, neglected and lopsided in a bare, hard-baked yard. It had a tin roof that curled at the corners and off to one side of it there stood what appeared to be an outside toilet constructed of sheets of weather-blackened metal.

Time and wear had had its effects on the house. Its two front windows were gone; squares of pasteboard had been nailed across their frames and its steps were rotted. It stood on block stilts and beneath it there was rubble—an old, decayed tarpaulin, broken bottles, a dented bucket, a wagon wheel with missing spokes. It was an ugly and desolate house; it's shame was relieved only by a row of porch plants—flowering red geraniums and pink begonias growing in rusted tin cans. "Those are mine," said Luke. "I brought them all the way from Colorado with me. I had a lot more but my dad got mad at me and threw 'em out." He was at the door, pulling it open and Ussy went in ahead of him.

They were in a small, rumpled room that smelled of sickness. There was a corner washstand containing a basin of soiled water, and clothes that had been worn hung from two overladen wall pegs. There was a table containing, on one end of it, the remnants of a meal —a pot of turnip greens and white bacon cooked together, some skillet-made cornbread, some slices of tomato. A portable cook stove setting on the other end of the table gave off a faint odor of kerosene.

A woman who was fully clothed lay on the bed in the corner. Her skin was the color of old wax. Luke went to her. "Mom? You awake?"

The woman opened her dark, fatigued eyes. "Oh, Luke. I didn't hear you come in."

"I brought Ussy, Mom. He can't stay but just a minute."

Luke's mother sat up. Her cotton dress was wrinkled and dirty. She put her bare feet on the floor and looked at Ussy. "Hello."

"Hello," said Ussy. The strange, helpless feeling

was at him again and he wasn't liking it. He bit his knuckles and tried to look interested. Who could be interested in what was here? All this dirt and mess. Luke's mother sure looked sick. Malaria wasn't contagious, was it? No, you got it from mosquitoes that carried it. Luke's mother could hardly weigh over eighty pounds. She needed a bath and some clean clothes. Why didn't Luke and his father clean up this place? Sure, it didn't belong to them but it was theirs for the present. Even a hole in the ground looked better when it was swept out. No, it needed more than sweeping. A broom wouldn't begin to touch the dirt; dirt everywhere and garbage and mess.

To his mother Luke was saying, "I went to the big house for some ice, Mom, but the truck hadn't come. It'll probably be here this afternoon sometime. If Dad'll let me off about two o'clock I'll go see about it again. Can you make out till then without it?"

Luke's mother had returned to her pillow. "Yes, it's all right."

"You want your medicine, Mom?"

"No, I took some just a little while ago."

"You think it's helping you?"

"I don't know. I suppose it is; it tastes bad enough."

"It's something with quinine in it," Luke explained to Ussy. "It makes her ears ring."

"I have to go," said Ussy. He didn't know if he should just leave or if he should try to say something else to Luke's mother. She looked awful. She had closed her eyes and pulled her rough sheet up around her. His visit hadn't accomplished a thing, not one thing. He was hungry and his head ached slightly and there was the whole afternoon before him.

Luke had pulled a box from beneath the table and was rummaging through its contents. "I need a piece of string to carry the ice with. Here are two little pieces; I guess I could tie them together. They might break though. You ever tried carrying twenty-five pounds of ice with just a piece of string for a handle?"

"No," confessed Ussy. "We have a refrigerator." The minute he said it he was sorry because it sounded like bragging. It wasn't; it was just the simple truth. At home there was always plenty of ice. He had never had to carry a piece of ice weighing twenty-five pounds. To him ice was an everyday thing. The refrigerator manufactured it faithfully; all he had ever had to do was open the door and reach in and get it.

Going back down the sand road to the dining hall Luke gently asked to borrow a quarter. "For the ice," he said. "The truck came this morning up at the big house but they wouldn't let me have it unless I paid for it right then and I didn't have any money. Neither did my dad. If you don't have a quarter maybe you could let me have just fifteen cents? I'll pay you back."

Ussy didn't think to ask when. In the face of the situation he couldn't very well haggle or refuse. Somehow he and other people like him had contributed to the way Luke and his family were. Somebody should be helping them or showing them how to help themselves. The people in the big house—they should be the ones. But they weren't doing it. They wouldn't even give Luke a quarter's worth of credit so he could buy ice for his sick mother. To have to live in that awful house back there. All in one room. There hadn't even been a bathroom. Where did they take their baths? In that tin shack out back probably. There hadn't even been a sink in the house. And Marsh, the brother next to Luke, had got himself adopted out in Colorado. That must have been a terrible thing for the other Wilders—to have to drive off and leave Marsh. Now the whole family was scattered. It was sure somebody's fault. It was a sin, that's what it was.

Ussy slipped his hand in his pocket and withdrew his last quarter. He handed it to Luke. The anxiety in him was the strangest feeling he had ever experienced. He heard himself speak low and urgently. "You don't have to pay this back, Luke. Just take it and get the ice for your mother. Don't worry about paying me back. I don't want you to."

It was the rightest thing he had ever done. He felt good about it all afternoon as he squatted in the hot sun, pulling and cutting his vegetables. He filled up his crates faster than the other boys who were dawdlers. He ate some carrots and some radishes; they didn't help his headache but still he felt good. He had done the right thing. He wouldn't go to Luke's house again; he didn't want anything more to do with Luke. He had his own problems and business to think and worry about. But it had been the right thing to do, to give Luke the quarter. He could afford it; now he was earning $4.50 a week.

CHAPTER SIX

After his first day of employment he sat with the members of his family at the supper table and was so agreeable and tolerant that they eyed him suspiciously. "How are things at the bank?" he asked his father.

"Oh, fine," answered Mr. Mock.

"I worked like a dog today," said Ussy. "But y'know, I'm not a bit tired." Loudly he complimented his mother on the excellence of her bread pudding which he detested. "This is so good!" he bellowed, shoveling great spoonsful of it into his mouth. "I just used to hate this stuff but now I love it. Isn't that funny? You must have done something different to it this time."

"No," said Mrs. Mock.

His grin embraced her and all the other members of his family. "It isn't my turn to do dishes tonight. Since I'm working and Winnie isn't I shouldn't have to do them any night but I don't mind doing more than my share. I'll do the dishes tonight if everybody will stay out of the kitchen while I'm doing them. I like privacy when I'm working."

"I think," said Ussy's father, "that I have misjudged you all these years. I am sorry."

"He's done something," said Winnie. "Or else he's getting ready to. Some of my friends are coming over after a while. Could he please be instructed to just mind his own business while they're here?"

"I won't bother your friends," said Ussy. "I won't even speak to them unless they speak to me first." His leg was killing him but it didn't need rest. What it needed was exercise so that it would stay limber.

He carried the dishes from the dining-room table to the laundry tub on the back porch and ran water over them. He filled the tub with hot water, added soap flakes, let them soak for ten minutes, pulled the plug and let them drain. He propped the back screen door open and dragged the garden hose in. He sprayed the dishes with the hose and let them air-dry. It was a new way toward greater efficiency in at least this one area of house drudgery. Maybe someday he'd invent a machine to do it better. He swept the kitchen, turned out the lights and went to the front porch. He chose the end that Winnie and her friends weren't using and sat alone for a few minutes—until Winnie remembered her company manners and invited him over.

One of Winnie's visitors was new in Medina. During the course of the evening Ussy found out that her name was Veronica Lovejoy, that she was from Memphis, Tennessee, had a father whose profession was drugless healing, that she could tap dance, yodel, play the violin better than Winnie, hated radio soap operas and knew the difference between a screw driver and a pair of pliers. She had great pansy eyes and a magnificent crown of jet black curls that hung stiffly from her head in long, glossy coils. She and her father traveled around the country by whatever means were handiest. He gave lectures and manufactured his own drugs known as Doctor Lovejoy's Golden Formulas which could cure halitosis, dropsy, liver ailments, colds, appendicitis, goiter, nervous headache, bronchitis, rapid heartbeat, thin blood, colic, too much acid in the system and not enough acid in the system.

Ussy almost fell in love with Veronica Lovejoy. She didn't shriek like the others when he showed them his rattlesnake head, and when he escorted them to his room, dragged his ghost from the closet, and said he'd try to make it leap and dart she didn't put her hands over her ears and run out.

"If it won't act like it's supposed to act there must be something wrong with it," said Veronica, peering and prying.

72

"Yes," said Ussy, gazing at her.

"I think I might see the trouble. You see this tiny little spring here underneath all the wires? It's come loose. Oh, there are a lot of springs and they're all loose. They should be connected to the wires. Do you have a pair of pliers?"

"Pliers?"

"And I'll need a screwdriver. A little one."

"A screwdriver," breathed Ussy and pressed one hand over his heart. The back of Veronica's neck was the cutest thing he had ever seen.

Veronica fixed his ghost. The others declined to watch it perform so he and Veronica took it out into the dark street and turned it loose. It danced and leaped and darted. It went behind a tree and collapsed and they ran to rescue it and wind its propelling mechanism again. Flapping grotesquely, it galloped around a corner, wobbled to a lamppost, and sank against it. Its skirt was black with dirt around the bottom and its face had come loose from its supporting wire frame; it hung in folds.

Gently Ussy gathered his ghost and he and Veronica sat on the curb beneath the lamppost. The yellow light from the lamp shining down upon them was on Veronica's hair and he wanted to touch it. He stroked the ghost in his lap and began to talk about himself in the queerest way. "I guess you know I'm employed."

"Yes," answered Veronica. "Winnie told me."

"It isn't much of a job; all I'm doing is picking

73

vegetables. But the way I figure it, a guy's got to start someplace."

"My father says work is honorable," murmured Veronica. "Any kind."

"Of course this isn't the first job I've ever had," said Ussy, gathering steam. "Coupla years ago I thought I might like to be a watchmaker so I tried that for a while. It was inside work though and I like to work outside so I gave it up."

"I like to be outside, too," said Veronica. "With nature. Nature is perfect. To work hard and be with nature, that is what my father always preaches. And drink lots and lots of water. Those are the first rules of health. And don't eat anything greasy. We use fish oil to cook with. I have never had a cold. How often do you have them?"

"Never," replied Ussy, the lie rippling from his tongue in the most startling way. Other lies followed it, tumbling out of his mouth so fast he scarcely recognized his own voice. He began to tell Veronica things he had never heard about or even thought of before. "Seems like I'm not like other guys. Never sick. I got some funny ideas about the way to live life, I guess. The way I see it you got to go out and grab it by its horns and pull. Know what I did a coupla years ago? I went over to Pensacola and got a job on a whaling vessel. I was the lookout. That's the guy who sits in the crow's nest and watches for whales. When he sees one he's supposed to holler, *Tharrrr sheeeee blowsssssssss!* Well, on the second day at sea I sighted a whole gam of them. Know what a gam is?"

74

Veronica shook her head. "No. I don't know what a crow's nest is either. You mean a nest for crows? Why would they have that on a whale boat?"

"A crow's nest isn't a nest for crows, Veronica. Not on a boat—a ship. On a ship it's a . . . it's a platform up on the mast. And a gam is a big bunch of whales. They're not fish; they're mammals. But they like to travel like fish. In schools. Veronica, I'll bet I'm the first guy you ever met who's been swallowed by a whale and lived to tell the story."

Veronica lifted her great pansy eyes to his. They glowed like diamonds. "Oh, no!"

"You mean I'm not? But I thought sure I was the first . . . in modern times, I mean. Of course I know there was Jonah . . . but I just don't see how anybody else could've beat me to it since him. . . . Veronica—"

"I meant to say yes," said Veronica. "Yes, you're the first person I've ever met who's been swallowed by a whale and lived to tell the story."

"Veronica, I was inside that whale for eight hours! Every time he swallowed or took a drink of water it was like a big storm passing through. It was an accident how I got inside him. I was up in the crow's nest and he was ramming the boat and the waves were coming over the side of it knocking everybody around and they were trying to get a harpoon in him. And all of a sudden he looked up at me and I lost my balance and fell. Right into his mouth. It was open. I almost was killed. I had to hook my belt around one of his teeth to keep from drowning. I was right up against his heart and I could feel it. *Booooom! Booooom! Booooom!*"

"My," said Veronica.

"Yes. Then the guys on the boat got a harpoon into him. The point of it just missed me by two inches. It nicked his heart and he rolled over and I fell down. He opened his mouth and his stomach filled up with water. I would've drowned if I hadn't been such a good swimmer. You like to swim?"

Veronica ducked her head. "No. I'm afraid of water. We used to spend our summers in Atlantic City and I would stand out on the boardwalk and look at the ocean. It's so deep and big. It scares me. I like land things."

"I could teach you how to swim," offered Ussy, thankful to be through with the whale story because it had run away with him. "There's nothing to it. All you got to remember to do is keep your feet and arms moving. I swim in Mullet River all the time; that's not very far from here. I could maybe rent a motorcycle and take you to Mullet River and teach you how to swim. I'm going to buy a motorcycle pretty soon. You ever rode on one?"

"No," replied Veronica. "They scare me. They go so fast and they make so much noise."

"I love motorcycles," declared Ussy. He was a man suddenly. He could feel manliness flowing through his bones and all his organs. It was so strong and strange. The feeling had never visited him before. He put his clenched fist to his mouth and bit his knuckles. Veronica had the prettiest set of knees, not bony one bit. An urge to please her rose in him. He would take her to see Mr. Suffrin, his history teacher. "Want

76

to meet somebody?" he said. "Mr. Suffrin, my history teacher. He lives . . . lessee . . . three blocks over. He's a funny old guy. No, not a guy; I shouldn't call him one. He's a teacher. When he talks to you about history you get mad you weren't born George Washington or Paul Revere or somebody like that. You can tell him anything. Let's go see him."

Veronica rose from the curb and did a little, clever jiggle dance on the sidewalk. She whirled away, skipping and jumping, avoiding the cracks in the sidewalks (because if she stepped on one it would bring bad luck) and a star fell, blazing a fiery trail, but it happened so fast neither of them had time to make a wish on it.

Mr. Suffrin's yard was cloistered in gray-black darkness. He was a willy-nilly landscaper; there were clumps of shaggy flowers and runners of gourd and melon vine. There was a row of corn and one of staked butter beans. There were purple eggplants, big as footballs, and tussocks of rough grass and several stalks of sugarcane. Mr. Suffrin's yard reflected his caprice and nimbleness—his funny way of running around being interested in all things all at one time. The door of his house was open and there was light streaming through it and all the windows were alight.

Mr. Suffrin was listening to music and making himself a new suit. "I figure to try everything once," he said, hopping around to sweep piles of books and magazines from chairs. "Suits in stores don't have much to offer a figure like mine and I can't afford a tailor so this afternoon I said to myself, Max, you should use your head for something besides a hat rack. So then I went out and bought this material . . . you like this color? I thought the stripe in it would make me look taller . . . and now, as you may see, I've taken this old suit apart for my pattern and cut a new one and already I've finished the pants, and when I've finished with the new one I'll put the old one back together again and then I'll have two. I borrowed this sewing machine. Now, Ussy, would you or wouldn't you say I'm a pretty clever fellow?"

"Sir," said Ussy. "I think you are a pretty clever fellow."

"What the world needs," declared Mr. Suffrin, "is more people like me and fewer people like Francisco Pasquale. That robber. I would be ashamed to tell you how much he charges to tailor a suit for a figure like mine. He only makes a teensy little bit of profit on them, he says. Meaning he wants me to think I have suddenly turned cracky and believe he works only for pleasure. What an actor. But I'll fool him and make my own suit. Look at this clever little pocket I have cut out to put in the vest. Pasquale charges extra for it but mine comes free. You see how I'm going to line it? With this little piece of satin. Tell me what you think of that, Master Ussy and Miss Veronica Lovejoy. Pretty clever, eh?"

"Pretty clever," said Ussy, meaning it.

"I like pockets in my clothes," said Veronica.

Mr. Suffrin sat at his borrowed sewing machine which had a foot treadle and furiously sewed two pieces of pin-stripe material together. "We could have tea," he suggested, "if somebody besides me would make it." But immediately the words were out of his mouth he forgot them. The machine being operated so fast made an awful racket and his scissors, lying beneath the material, bounced up and down and clattered to the floor and Veronica ran from her chair to retrieve them and though Mr. Suffrin's seam was puckered in spots and a little zig-zaggy he was immodestly pleased with it. "If you would like to know the trouble with the world today I will tell you," he said. "It is man's dependence on his fellow man. We have ceased to think and act for ourselves. We cannot perform our own simplest services any more but must run to the specialist for every little thing."

"Excuse me," said Veronica. "Mr. Suffrin—"

"I tell you," said Mr. Suffrin, holding his half-completed garment up to the light, "dependence on others goes quite a little against my grain. Why should I have to depend on Pasquale to make me a suit when I can make such a beautiful one myself? Know what I'm going to do when I've finished it? I'm going to make a little embroidered label that says Tailored by Max Suffrin and sew it just inside the lapel so that when the coat flaps open people will see it. Pasquale will turn green with envy when I show it to him. He will cry."

Veronica had forgotten what she had been going to say to Mr. Suffrin. She was fascinated with his antics, the way he drooped one eyelid during a moment of perplexity and crawled around on all fours looking for dropped pins and snip-snipped three sleeves, depriving his suit of half a vest. He draped a strip of the suit material across the top of his head so as not to forget where it was but it kept slipping down so he tied it in a bow under his chin. His music played and he hummed and treadled his sewing machine and chattered. During the last minutes of the visit he again remembered to offer refreshment but then sadly discovered there were only a few leaves in the bottom of the canister. "Then you will have an eggplant instead," he said, "to take home and cook and enjoy." And rushed to the yard and wrenched two from their stems.

Walking Veronica home, Ussy said, "Nobody but him would have ever thought of giving us eggplants for presents. Isn't that funny? He's why I make better grades in history than any other subject."

"He's funny," said Veronica, jumping over the cracks in the sidewalk. "But I don't think I'd want him for my teacher. He doesn't look like a teacher. Or act like one."

Ussy shifted his ghost from one arm to the other and the head of it fell down, dangling against his knee. Veronica's dainty little feet in their little slippers flashed white in the darkness and her saucy little skirt lifted with each movement of her round little legs in the cutest way. Only he didn't think she was so cute any more. Veronica, he reflected, had an imagination that was duller than dishwater. She didn't have any, that was her trouble. She just wasn't any too bright if she didn't like Mr. Suffrin. Even if she did know how to fix ghosts.

80

CHAPTER SEVEN

He had a job and his seal of independence—his beautiful tattoo. And he knew what his goals were. They were to overthrow the obstacles of home and family and take his life in his own hands and have it for his own. They were to hoard his money, buy a motorcycle, get on it and roar westward, free as a sparrow. He would work his way across the southern plains, sleeping in nice, sweet-smelling haystacks. In New Orleans he would tarry long enough to sit in a sidewalk cafe and drink a little cup of black, syrupy coffee. (New Orleans was one of Mr. Suffrin's favorite places.) In

San Antonio, Texas, he'd stop and look at the Alamo. (Every American should see this historic building, occupied by brave Texas volunteers during a battle with a Mexican army in 1836.) When he got to San Francisco, Gateway to the Orient, he would rent himself a nice room from a little old lady who would promise not to ever snoop through his stuff, open his mail, tell him what to think, or make any decisions for him. He'd make his own decisions. His dreams would be his private property; he'd dream what he felt like dreaming and never have to relate them to anybody unless he felt like it.

He'd steer clear of people like Luke Wilder who was a real pain in the whatzis. On the second day of Ussy's being an employee on the Snyder farm Luke again asked him to smuggle meat out to him from the noon table and because he wasn't prepared to refuse —hadn't had the foresight to think of an advance excuse—he was obliged to again go against one of Packy's rules.

The two little patties of hamburger, wrapped in Ussy's paper napkin, nettled and distressed Luke. "Aw, now, what's this? I thought you was having pork chops. Up at the big house they are."

"It's hamburger," said Ussy.

"Yeah," said Luke. "I can see that. It's got bread in it. They cheated. You didn't have pork chops?"

"No, Luke, I didn't have pork chops. I had hamburger patties, same as those. I got to go back now. Packy'll be blowing his whistle any minute."

Luke devoured the meat patties. His dull, tousled

82

hair hung down thick and black over the sides of his soiled face. His clothes were stiff with dirt. The laces of his tennis shoes were gone. He gave off a strong, foul smell. Ussy wanted away from him but Luke was moving toward him, grinning, extending his hand, showing him the watch in the palm of it. "Aw, you got almost half an hour. See, I still got the watch. I thought you'd ask me how my mother was. Don't you want to know?"

Ussy started to bite his knuckles but changed his mind. He put his hands in his pockets. His pay from the prior day's work was there in the right one—a nice, fat, shiny silver dollar. He slid his thumb and forefinger over it. He liked the feel of it. "Of course, I want to know how your mother is," he said. "But we were just so busy talking about the meat. How is she?"

Luke didn't answer him at once. They had gone around to the end of the dining-hall building to make the transaction with the meat patties a private thing and now Luke went over and leaned against the wall. He was so thin and dirty and friendless. His grin had faded and the lids of his eyes were down. He sighed. "My mother," he said, "is very sick. Very sick. She needs the doctor again but he won't come without the money. She needs ice every day and milk and fruit. Other things, too. Maybe she'll die."

"She won't," said Ussy. The silver dollar was thick between his thumb and forefinger and there was a thread of anxiety forming in the cage of his ribs. He wasn't sure at all that Luke's mother wouldn't die.

"My dad doesn't know what to do about her," said

Luke after a moment. "All he knows how to do is drive a truck."

"Well," said Ussy, "that doesn't sound right to me. He's got to know other things, too. Your dad should go to Packy or somebody. He should borrow some money from somebody."

Luke stared at the ground. "He did. He went to Packy and now we owe all of next month's salary. If we didn't, Packy would make us leave. He and my dad don't get along very good. You've seen what a temper Packy's got."

"Yes," said Ussy and the thread of anxiety running back and forth between his ribs softened to sympathy. He was being drawn into Luke's trouble.

It was very true that Packy had a temper. Early that morning Luke's father had stalled his truck—had misjudged a turn and run into an irrigation ditch. Some of the loaded crates on the back of it had been thrown off to the ground and it had taken quite a while to get everything righted again with Packy running up and down shouting directions and insults and Luke's father trying to obey all of Packy's orders at one time. Luke's father hadn't had much to say but Packy had plenty to say:

"Stupid! Don't you know an irrigation ditch when you see one? You're wasting time, man! My time! Back it up! Back it! Well, go forward then! Do something! Don't just sit there, stupid!"

Luke's father was a slight, stooped man, smaller than Packy but capable of the same feelings. After the truck had been freed of the ditch and all the crates of vegetables loaded again he had driven away hating Packy. It had shown in his pale eyes and the set of his mouth. The hatred was deserved. No grown man should be called stupid in front of a bunch of kids.

Luke's father owed Packy his next month's wages and Luke's mother had malaria. People could die from malaria. Yes, they could. It was an old, historical disease. Mr. Suffrin had spoken of it in his history class —severe epidemics of it in the Americas as far back as 1493.

The coin in his pocket was only one day's salary. It was only money. He couldn't just stand there and pretend that the little bit of help it would buy wasn't within his power. Slowly Ussy withdrew the silver dollar and went over to Luke. "Here. Take this money and buy some ice for your mother."

Luke raised his eyes. He turned his head and stared out across the fields. "I don't know when I could pay you back."

"Did I ask you to pay me back? Take it."

"I can't. It's not right."

"Take it."

"No."

"Take it."

"I can't. I shouldn't have told you what I did. It isn't your worry what happens to us."

"Take it I said! And buy your mother some ice. Tomorrow I'll bring her some fruit. I know there's not enough here for that and the doctor and all. Luke, you going to take this money or not?"

Luke turned and silently, humbly held out his

hand. Ussy pressed the silver dollar into the palm of it and all he could notice was the dirt on the inside of Luke's wrist. It wasn't fresh dirt; it looked like it had been there a long time. Luke's shirt and pants were too big for him. For his age he should be bigger than he was. It occurred to Ussy that he didn't know Luke's age. He asked it. "Luke, how old are you?"

Luke's bright, boy's grin was quick. It proffered trust and established something between them. "Thirteen," he answered. "But you're the onliest one here knows it. Packy thinks I'm sixteen. That's how old I'm supposed to be to work here and not go to school regular."

One part of Ussy's life ended that day. Late in the afternoon he was returned to his home in Medina via the transport truck and when he went up the steps of the front porch and saw and smelled all the safe, familiar things a change took place in him. The Mock house was more comfortable than it had the right to be, so clean and cool and big. White curtains shining with starch, fresh, cut flowers in a bowl on the dining-room sideboard, the white, clean kitchen with the big, white refrigerator. Skinny-Winnie was in the kitchen making peanut butter fudge. She wore a clean, pink dress and had a pink silk scarf tied around her head. She smelled like wave-set lotion.

He trudged past her and went to the refrigerator for milk. He drank it from the bottle. Skinny-Winnie frowned at this but didn't say anything. He leered at her.

"Fudge again, huh? Don't you ever think about anything besides your gut?"

Happy in her little role of housewifery, she smiled at him. "What's the matter with you? Oooooh, you stink. Go take a bath."

He stood in front of her, glaring. She was beating the warm, fragrant syrup, watching it closely. Whether it would or would not thicken was her only worry. "Some people don't even have sugar to put in their coffee," he said. "Some people don't even have any coffee. You ever stop to think about that?"

"My, my, my," said Winnie.

"Yeah. And all you can think about is your own gut. Why are you so useless? Why don't you go out and get a job and learn how to support yourself?"

"I'm not ever going to support myself," said Winnie. "Women don't have to. That's what men are for. That's the way the world is. Sorry you don't like it, Uss. But it's not my fault, really it isn't."

Trapped in this truth he leaned against the refrigerator door. Old Skinny-Winnie was about the same size as Luke's mother. Fatter. But up and down they were about the same size. "What do you do with your old clothes?" he demanded.

The fudge had hardened to the right consistency. Winnie poured it from the pan on to her two buttered platters. "Mama gives them to the church."

"What does the church do with 'em?"

"They give them to the needy."

"Any particular needy?"

"The needy in our church congregation, Ussy.

You wouldn't have to ask me that if you ever paid attention to some of the things you're supposed to. If church wasn't just a joke to you."

It was another truth; he couldn't deny it. He hunched his shoulders forward trying to release the ache in them. "Well," he said, "I don't want to have to go to the church and ask."

"Ask for what?" inquired Skinny-Winnie. She was being superior because she was clean and rested and happy and he was dirty and tired and was letting the fact that he had a little problem show.

"The old clothes," he said. "I can't go down to the church and ask for them. I don't want to. I just want you to give me some of your old clothes. You've got a whole closet full. It won't hurt you to give a few of 'em away."

"But I just told you," said Skinny-Winnie. "Mama gives all our old clothes to the church. Now with whom have you gotten yourself involved, Ussy? What is it this time?"

He wanted to laugh. Old Skinny-Winnie just always had to be coy about things. She was always so right and good. But he needed the clothes, at least one dress and maybe a slip. He forced himself to pleasantry. "There's this family living on the Snyder farm," he began.

"What family, Ussy?"

"I'm trying to tell you. Their name is Wilder and the mother's got malaria—"

"Do they belong to our church, Ussy?"

"I don't know. No, I don't think so. I don't think

they go to any church. I didn't ask. But that's got nothing—"

"They should go to church," said Winnie. "Everybody should."

"Mrs. Wilder needs some clothes," said Ussy. "She's about your size. She's very sick."

"Their church would help them," said Winnie. "If they belonged to one."

He wondered what would happen if he just went over to her, raised his fist and socked her a couple of times on her pure jaw. She'd scream and yell, that's what would happen and in the end he wouldn't have accomplished anything for the Wilders. He took a deep breath. "Winnie, it makes no difference whether these people I'm telling you about go to church or not. I'll tell them they should go if they don't already. But first this woman I'm telling you about has got to have some clothes. She's lying out there in a dress so filthy you wouldn't scrub a hog with it and she's sick and you ought to see this place where they have to live and the father owes Packy Snyder all of his next month's salary —"

"Packy Snyder? Who's Packy Snyder?"

"He's Mr. Snyder's nephew. You know. Mr. Snyder. At the bank where our father works?"

"These people," said Winnie, "should join our church. Our church helps all its needy members. You should tell them that, Ussy." Her eyes were wide and pure and unyielding. She wasn't going to give him any clothes for Mrs. Wilder. She said, "Why do you always have to be the hero, Ussy?"

"Hero?" said Ussy. "I'm no hero."

"You like people to think you are. I saw Veronica Lovejoy today. She told me that whale story. You're ridiculous, Ussy. Just ridiculous. The least you could have done was pick a southern fish. Whales are northern fish; they don't come this far south."

"Whales aren't fish," said Ussy. "They're mammals."

"And another thing, Ussy. There was a man here this morning looking for somebody named Casper Bismuth Nestley."

"Who's Casper Bismuth Nestley?"

"Ussy, how should I know? He's somebody seventy-two years old who's interested in taking an art course. This man from Minneapolis—"

"What man from Minneapolis?"

"The man selling the art courses, Ussy. He travels all over the country selling art courses. His company sends out applications to people they think might be interested in art courses and if they fill them out and send them back then this man goes to see them when he's in their town. He's here in Medina now staying at the Medina Hotel. He came out here this morning looking for Casper Bismuth Nestley. I told him we didn't know any Casper Bismuth Nestley and he showed me a paper that somebody had filled out and mailed to his company's office that said Pody Mock had told Casper Bismuth Nestley about the art course."

Ussy shoved himself away from the refrigerator door. He stood in front of it for a moment, his arms dangling loosely. He hooked his thumbs in his belt and with uninterrupted fixity gazed at Winnie. "Casper Bismuth Nestley sounds like a jerk to me. If he's seventy-two years old and wants to take an art course there must be something wrong with him. Do you think he lives around here?"

"Nobody knows, Ussy. The art man is going to phone you."

"Phone me? What for?"

"Oh, he thinks you might know who Casper Bismuth Nestley is."

"I don't," said Ussy. "When that guy from Minneapolis phones, you can just tell him for me I don't know any Casper Bismuth Nestley. And tell him don't bother me. Tell him I'm busy."

Ussy went to the bathroom, locked the door, and shed his clothes. He filled the tub with water as hot as he could stand it and got in. He scrubbed the dirt from his face, hair, and body. He let the first water run out and filled the tub again. Beneath the layer of the clear, shimmering water his tattoo was beautiful. He lay in the clean water for a long time; until it cooled. He heard the phone in the hall ringing and then Winnie's footsteps just outside the bathroom door. She yelled to him. "Ussy?"

"What d'you want?"

"The art man from Minneapolis wants to talk to you!"

"Tell him I don't want to talk to him!" screamed Ussy. "Tell him I'm taking a bath!"

"Ussy, Mama says for you to get out of that tub and talk to the art man!"

"Aw, zounds!" said Ussy and got out of the tub, wrapped a towel around him, opened the bathroom door and trotted to the phone. He spoke to the man from Minneapolis softly. "Hello."

"Hello," said the art man. "Is this Casper Bismuth Nestley?"

"No, sir. This is Ussy Mock."

"Oh," said the art man. "I thought it was Casper Bismuth Nestley."

"No, sir," said Ussy. "This here is Ussy Mock. You must have the wrong number."

"Oh," said the art man sadly. "I guess I must have. But maybe you can help me."

"Sir?"

"I'm looking for a man named Casper Bismuth Nestley—"

"I don't know anybody by the name of Casper Bismuth Nestley—"

"Are you sure? He's seventy-two years old and lives at 323 Avenue of Beauty."

"Sir, I don't know anybody seventy-two years old living at 323 Avenue of Beauty."

"I've been all over town looking for this person," said the art man. "But I can't find him. I can't even find his street. Nobody seems to know where 323 Avenue of Beauty is."

"I never heard of it," said Ussy, sweating a little. "Or Casper Bismuth Nestley neither. I live at 323 Monroe Street."

"Yes, I know that," said the art man. "I was at your home this morning and talked to your lovely mother and sister. Your little brother, too. He's certainly a bright youngster."

"Yes, sir. I like him."

"It seems odd to me," said the art man, "that I can't locate this Casper Bismuth Nestley. I've combed this town. I even inquired at the Chamber of Commerce and the bank. I guess it was your father I spoke with at the bank."

Ussy allowed himself to lean against the telephone table. He was sweating freely now. After a moment he said, "Well, I guess you're just going to have to give up on finding your man then. Maybe you've got the wrong town."

"No," said the art man. "I've got the envelope he mailed his application in right in front of me. It's postmarked Medina. You don't think the post office would make a mistake and put their postmark on a piece of mail that hadn't gone out of here, do you?"

"I don't know," answered Ussy, beginning to feel desperate. "I don't know anything about the post office. I guess they could make a mistake and —"

"Would you do me a favor?"

"Favor? What kind?"

"Would you," said the art man, "just kind of think about Casper Bismuth Nestley for a while?"

"You want me to think about Casper Bismuth Nestley? What for? What I mean is . . . I don't *mind* thinking about him but I don't know what good . . . what I mean is, how can I think about him if I don't know him?"

"You might remember him after you've had time to think about him for a while," said the art man, gently persuasive. "If something comes to your mind about him you could phone me at the Medina Hotel. I'm going in to have my supper now but after that I'll be in my room. I'll look forward to hearing from you."

"Yes," said Ussy. "Yes. Yes. I'll phone you if something comes to me." And hung up the phone without getting the art man's name. He went to his room and dressed himself in fresh clothing. He brushed his hair and smoothed his eyebrows. At the last minute he put on a necktie. His father had come home and the evening meal was being put on the table. Ussy went from his room and joined his family.

The hot, good food, the quiet comfort of eating his last meal of the day with his family lulled him to a sense of false security. His little joke on the art course people had unbelievably caught up with him but nothing was going to come of it. The man from Minneapolis would probably just eat his own supper and maybe take a little walk and then go to bed. He had to be something of a jerk. To go running around all over Medina looking for a jerk like Casper Bismuth Nestley who didn't even exist. He sounded young and like he had plenty of energy. Probably he was the son of the president of the art course company—a guy like Packy Snyder who had always had everything handed to him. It'd do him good not to be able to locate Casper Bismuth Nestley. Serve him right. He and his father would maybe think twice the next time they got ready to send out their silly applications to people who hadn't even asked for them. The world was a big enough mess without people cluttering up the United States mails with more.

Ussy sat with his family at the Mock supper table and tried to look alert and interested and casual. His father eyed his necktie and wanted to know if he had plans for the evening and he jerked to attention and said, "No. I just put this on to eat supper in. A guy's neck looks better with a tie around it, don't you think so?"

There was blueberry pie with whipped cream for dessert and Winnie cut him an extra large piece. He was halfway through it when the phone rang. His father went to answer it and came back to the dining room to say, "Phone, Ussy."

The last morsel of his pie slid down his throat into his stomach. He laid his fork down on his plate. Everybody was watching him, his father most of all. He left his chair and went to the phone in the hallway. He held the instrument to his ear. "Hello? This is Ussy Mock. Who's this?"

"I was just wondering," said the art course man from Minneapolis, "if anything had jogged your memory concerning Casper Bismuth Nestley."

"No," said Ussy, sweating. "Like I told you before, I never heard of him."

"If you want to know what I honestly think," said the art man, slowly and lazily, "I think you aren't being honest with me. I think you know *all* about Casper Bismuth Nestley. I think he's there with you. In your house. I wish you'd let me speak to him."

"I can't," said Ussy, his voice rising. He shook the phone. "I told you I never heard of him! What—"

"Come on now. Let me speak to him. I just want to—"

"I told you he ain't here! I can't make him here if he ain't! Can I?"

"I just want to speak to him for one itty-bitty minute. You see, he's seventy-two years old—"

"He ain't either!" screamed Ussy.

"He ain't? How do you know that if you don't know him? Is he there? Did he come? Let me speak to him."

"He ain't here!" shrieked Ussy, shaking the phone. "Can't you understand that? He ain't here! Casper Bismuth Nestley ain't here! He's not seventy-two years old and he ain't here! Hang up! Let me alone!"

All the members of his family had come to stand in the hall doorway. They were watching him. Hugging the phone to his ear, Ussy turned his back on them. There was a long minute of silence on the line and then the art man said, "Well, all right then. Sorry to have bothered you."

"You didn't bother me," babbled Ussy. "Not one bit." And then in one of his truest rushes of honesty said, "Mister, Casper Bismuth Nestley is dead. What I mean is, I made him up. He was never alive."

"Well," said the art man. "I will be jiggered."

"So I'm sorry and good-bye," said Ussy.

"Goooood-bye," sang the art man.

Ussy put the phone back in its cradle. His father asked, "Wrong number, Uss?"

"No," replied Ussy. "It was a . . . a mistake I made. It's finished now. I hope."

Mortified and chastised he sat alone on the front porch steps until it was fully dark. Except for an occasional passing car no sound disturbed the neighborhood. The peace of it rasped his nerves.

The business concerning Casper Bismuth Nestley made him forget about the Wilders until after he went to bed. He lay in the cool, dark room and sleep came almost immediately but then some small outside noise jerked him wide awake. His sheets were smooth, the noise had only been the wind rattling a tree branch, the friendly, visiting moon was at his window and yet he could not sleep. He lay making some plans for the coming day. He would snitch what fruit there was in the refrigerator, take it to Luke and say, "This is all I can do for you, Luke. I got my own canoe to paddle. I was going to ask my father and mother to help but something came up. Anyway, they aren't rich. My father has to work like a dog to keep us. If we have anything left over my mother gives it to the church. Churches help people. Why don't you join one? I can't help you any more, Luke. I got my own troubles. You don't have to pay me back that dollar and a quarter. It was a present. Good-bye."

And that would be the end of that. Maybe he should take the Wilders a couple of bars of bath soap.

A box of laundry soap, too. His mother always kept a good supply of both kinds.

Ussy rose from his bed and went through the silence and the darkness of the house to the kitchen. Without turning on a light he opened the cabinet next to the refrigerator and found two bars of bath soap and a box of soap powder. In the morning he'd get what fruit there was in the refrigerator. He'd leave the house early, before his mother got up. He'd meet the transport truck down at the corner of his street. He'd explain to his mother about the fruit and the soap. He'd pay her for it with his own money.

Ussy returned to his room and bed and slept for two hours. Then he was wide awake again. He lay thinking of Turner and Directly and how he would, at summer's end, make his escape from Medina and go to San Francisco and find them. San Francisco was a big place but he'd find his friends; he would.

Ussy smiled to himself and rearranged his pillow. He closed his eyes and slept.

CHAPTER EIGHT

On the third day of his employment with Medina's Summer Work Camp for Boys he did not see Luke until noon. All morning he toiled in the fiery sun, digging and cutting and pulling the vegetables. His legs ached from squatting and he sweated until his clothes were wet, even his socks. The radishes were the worst. The tops of these were prickly and stung his sunburned hands and wrists. There was a certain satisfaction in the small pain of this. He wasn't yet a man but he was doing a man's work. Let the boys in the rows up ahead of him and across from him and behind him play. They cheated, stuffing wadded newspaper in the bottoms of their crates and throwing the vegetables in on top to make the crates look full. They did a lot of horsing around. There was always something wrong with one of them; a bite or scratch or a cut. They grumbled about the work conditions and argued with Packy about them. During the rest periods they had water fights and fist fights and vandalized the rest-building. They punched the screens of its windows out and carved their initials and four-lettered words on its newly painted walls. Two of the worst offenders quit the project at Packy's invitation. The dirt and the heat and the discipline had been just too much for them. They were sissies.

The dirt didn't bother him so long as he knew he could wash it off when his work was done. It was just earth and he was a part of the earth; he had always been a part of it. How could anyone not feel this? Everybody was.

It was a Wednesday. All Wednesdays were a half-holiday. Everything in Medina, including the bank, always closed at noon on Wednesdays. What would he do with the useless afternoon? At home it would be deadly with Winnie's radio programs and his mother and father puttering around. Maybe he would go to see Mr. Suffrin; they would talk about what was going on in Europe. Hitler's Nazis killing the Jews and all that stuff.

Kneeling in the black dirt, Ussy pulled his radishes and filled his crates. Working the rows that had been assigned to him he moved back and forth on his knees because it was quicker and more efficient that way; it was painful to stand up every time he finished with one area. The sun was blinding and he tasted the dirt between his teeth.

A cast of hawks flew over his head, wings whistling. They settled in the spindly pines that ringed the truck gardens. He smelled the delicious fragrance of sweet-bay drifting in from the hammocks beyond the pines. Mr. Wilder came alone in his truck for a load of the crates and again ran across an irrigation ditch and got stuck and Packy appeared, flapping his arms and screaming. "Idiot! Nobody but an idiot makes the same mistake in two days running! What's the matter with you? Can't you see? Are you blind?"

Mr. Wilder's head was shaking as if from palsy. He got out of his truck and walked around it. He leaned to examine the back wheels which were sunken to the hubs in black, wet mud. "It's stuck," he observed. "Stuck good this time. I just didn't see it. I just sure didn't."

"Well, get it out!" shrieked Packy. "It isn't going to come out by itself! Don't just stand there! Get it out!"

Mr. Wilder dropped to all fours and examined his problem. He stood up, looked once at Packy, went around the truck, got in and started it. One back wheel of it spun; it merely sprayed mud. Mr. Wilder got out of the truck and came back to Packy. "It's not gonna come out, Packy. I can't get it out by myself. Maybe some of your boys could give me a hand. Maybe a few of 'em could get up there in the front and give me a little push and I could try backin' her out."

Packy's Adam's apple had escaped his collar. The rest of his neck was burned deep brown from the sun; his Adam's apple was queerly pale. "No," he said. "I can't allow that. Somebody might get hurt. These boys are special; you know that."

"Then what—?" asked Mr. Wilder.

"Where's your helper?" demanded Packy. "Where's Luke?"

"Uh," said Mr. Wilder. "He wasn't feelin' so good this morning. I told him to stay home till noon."

"It's noon now," said Packy. "I don't see him. Where is he?"

Mr. Wilder put his right fingers in the palm of his left hand and squeezed. "It's Wednesday, Packy. Wednesday's a half-holiday. 'Member?"

Packy shot his cuffs. "All right, all right. But what about this truck? You can't let it just set there. After these boys have had their lunch you've got to get them back to town. And there's still a full load of stuff here to be taken to the wash sheds. So what about it, Wilder?"

"I'll get it out," said Luke's father. The hate for Packy was in his eyes. He leaned against the rear fender of the truck. "You're gettin' two for the price of one, Packy. Me and Luke. Both for the wages of one. And I'm using my truck. Just don't push your luck too far. Even a man in the straits I'm in has got pride."

"I'm furnishing you a house to live in," said Packy. "And I'm paying you ten dollars a month extra for the use of your truck and I'm buying gas and oil for it. Now if the conditions of our agreement are beginning to set not so well with you, you can leave, Wilder. Nobody's holding you here by force."

A look of pride and hopeful doubt went swiftly across Mr. Wilder's soiled, country face. "I owe you, Packy. I'm not forgettin' that. I never walked out on no debt."

"I meant after you've worked out what you owe me, Wilder. In the meantime what about this truck?"

Mr. Wilder was pulling his cap down; the stained, limp bill of it hid his eyes. "I'll get it out. Don't worry about it. You and your boys go on and have your dinner. I'll get 'em back to town. I'll get this truck out. I'll get all your stuff to the wash sheds. I'll pay you what I owe you—work it out. Don't worry about it. Just you go on and do what you got to do and I'll do what I got to do and we'll get along."

Packy contained his disbelief and contempt for the older man's promise. He turned away from Mr. Wilder, put his whistle to his lips and blew. It was noon.

On the way to the dining-hall building Ussy saw Luke. The rest of the boys and Packy were ahead of him walking briskly, some of the boys with their heads together laughing and talking. They were glad to be released for the day. Sammy Hicks, the dirty-joke teller, was walking beside Packy, was ingratiating himself to the supervisor. Sammy's round, firm bottom muscled with each step he took. He was vastly proud of the way he was built. His ambition was to become a varsity football player. He'd make it, too, rah, rah,

rah. In the classroom Sammy was duller than dishwater but already on the gridiron he was a champion. He was sometimes allowed to practice with older boys and nobody could stop him when he got the ball. His long, muscled legs carried him to the goal post as if they were powered by a great, artificial force. He took two different vitamin pills every day and drank twelve glasses of water. Everybody in his family did this. Sammy's teeth were so perfectly white they looked artificial but they weren't and his lips were so red they looked like he wore lipstick but he didn't. Almost everybody liked Sammy—he was so full of energy and fun—Ussy didn't. He hated Sammy's jokes and the way he looked at girls and the way he walked, jutting his hips from side to side. Nobody walked like that naturally.

Following Packy and Sammy and the other boys down the dirt road that led to the dining building, Ussy tried to imitate Sammy's walk but it was just too much trouble. His hip bones hurt and there was pain between his shoulder blades and he felt as if he were melting. After the noon meal had been eaten Packy would have everybody line up for their pay. Then they'd be taken back to Medina. He'd leave the truck before it reached his home. Maybe instead of going to see Mr. Suffrin he'd go to the woods. If he could muster the energy to walk that far maybe he'd go to Mullet River for a swim; find a shallow place in it and just sit and let the water wash over him. He'd stay all afternoon in the coolness there. There was no sense in the weather being this hot.

Ussy tasted the gritty, black dirt that was between

his teeth and followed the others who were taking a shortcut, abandoning the road to go through a palmetto barren. They were intent only on reaching the dining hall and the food that waited for them there. They did not see Luke who came silently and suddenly through the scrub. Parting the palmettos he stepped out of them and came toward Ussy. Ussy stopped walking and Luke came up to him. "Hiya. Where you going?"

"To lunch," answered Ussy and wanted to run after Packy and the others. "And then we're all going home because it's Wednesday." He forced his voice to a bright casual pitch. "I brought the fruit for your mother and a couple other things. They're in a sack in the building where we have our rest periods. I put them under one of the cots. Could you go get them? By yourself? I have to go eat lunch."

Luke was scrubbing at his eyes with his fists. His same, dirty clothes were dirtier than ever, stiff with old dirt and greasy. He chose to explain himself. "I think I've got a little touch of malaria. I was a little bit sick this morning. That's why I wasn't out working with my dad. I thought you'd forget the fruit. Anybody else would have. What other things did you bring?"

"Soap," said Ussy. "I thought you might like some. Look, Luke, I've got to go now. You'll go get the stuff, won't you?"

Lonely and despaired, Luke hung his head. "I'll go get it. The fruit'll be good. We haven't had any for a long time. I remembered it was Wednesday. I thought after you'd had your dinner you could come to my house for a while."

"No," said Ussy and began to grab at quick excuses. "I have to eat my lunch first—"

"I know that. I'll wait for you."

"Then I have to get paid—"

"That won't take long."

"It'll take a while. I don't know why Packy pays us every day except that guys are always dropping out of the project."

"You're the onliest one here that's been friendly to me," said Luke. "You were so good about giving me the money for my mother and bringing me stuff left over from what you ate. So I thought what I'd do is try and pay you back a little bit. I thought you could come to my house after you ate and we could talk and . . . and I've got something real interestin' to show you."

"Luke, I've got my own plans—"

"It's an armadillo. You ever seen one?"

"No, I don't think so."

"My dad and I caught him last night. I thought you'd like to see him. I wasn't so crazy about catching him. I wouldn't have worked so hard at catching him except I thought you'd like to see him. I thought you'd be interested. I never thought you wouldn't be. You seemed different than the others."

"Luke, I *am* different than the others but you got to understand."

"There's a panther out there where we live. We can hear it cryin' sometimes at night. Like a woman.

Last night we heard it and I was afraid but I went after the armadillo anyway because I thought you'd like him. Now you don't."

"I like him," protested Ussy. "I've only seen pictures of them. I know I'd like him. Honest. But didn't you just hear me? I've got to go eat. Then I've got to get paid. Then I've got to go back to Medina with the rest of them."

Luke said nothing. His eyes were red from rubbing them. His twisted smile conveyed his gentle hurt. Now he was patient and wistfully forgiving. He wasn't going to ask for anything more or offer anything more. He let his back slump and locked his hands in front of him; dejectedly he regarded them. He stood silent and disappointed, not waiting for Ussy to speak again, not waiting for anything.

The feeling of guilt and helplessness that Luke's presence always brought to him was overflowing in Ussy's stomach. In some way not clear to him or explainable he felt flawed. How Luke was—his dirtiness and loneliness and want—had nothing to do with him. There was so much trouble everywhere: the Jews in Europe being murdered by Hitler and the big financial depression in the United States. So much trouble and misery. Why did he have to be aware of all the trouble and misery? He was going to stop reading the newspaper and listening to the news on the radio. It wasn't doing him or anybody else any good. He couldn't help any of it. He was just one person. Ussy bit his knuckles. In some queer way he was responsible for and involved in the things that were wrong with Luke.

Packy and the others were out of sight and out of earshot now. There was just himself and Luke and Luke's problem. Well, it really wasn't a problem. He could handle it. He could go on and have his lunch and get paid, go and spend thirty minutes or so with Luke and then have the rest of the afternoon free. There remained the question of how he would get back to Medina. It was a brightening thought. Ussy said, "After I eat and get paid I guess I could go to your house and see the armadillo. But then I wouldn't have any way to get home."

Luke had the answer to that. His face cleared. "I thought about that. I've already got you a ride back to Medina. The cook from the big house always goes in about two o'clock on Wednesday to visit some of his friends. I've already got you a ride with him."

It was his own fault. He should have told Luke the plain truth—should have remembered the little speech he had designed the night before—that he had his own canoe to paddle, that he had done for Luke all he could do. Now the time was gone. At least temporarily it was. To have to give some of his free afternoon to somebody he merely felt sorry for wasn't fair but it was his own fault. It would teach him to be a little more careful with his sympathy.

Comradely again and eager, Luke was saying, "While you're having your dinner I'll go get the fruit and stuff from the rest-building. Then I'll come back and wait for you outside. Up at the big house they're having fried chicken for their dinner. It sure smelled good. Ussy—"

"You don't have to ask me," said Ussy quickly. "If we have fried chicken I'll bring you a piece. I'll bring you something." He didn't want to hear Luke ask him for that. He felt old and heavy.

The armadillo was dead and this was a shock because he had expected to see a live one but the Wilders had killed and dressed it for eating. One of them had used a sharp knife to remove the animal from his thick, bony shell. The feet and long, triangular head had been removed, the breast bones and pelvic bones had been cut through to allow removal of the entrails, fat, and sweat glands. The tail had been severed. Now this piece of flesh, weighing maybe five or seven pounds, lay on a wrinkled brown paper on the Wilders' eating table. The air and the paper beneath it had absorbed a good deal of its moisture; it looked tough and leathery. Mrs. Wilder was in her bed against the wall. Her eyes were closed and she had the rough sheet drawn up around her shoulders.

"She's not really asleep," said Luke pushing the armadillo's discarded head, feet, tail, and armor from the straight chair. "She's just resting. She's weak from the malaria. It comes and goes."

"You should give her a piece of fruit," suggested Ussy. "It'd probably taste good to her."

Luke had the bag open containing the fruit and the soap. He was peering into it. "I will in a minute. Apples and bananas. Gee." He grinned at Ussy and pointed to the carcass of the armadillo. "Didn't I tell you I had a armadillo? We're going to eat him for our supper tonight. If he can get some from Packy, Dad's going to stuff him with some sweet potatoes. That's how we used to fix 'em when we lived in Texas. I've been eating them all my life. Sit down, why don't you?"

The cabin was suffocatingly hot. Reluctantly Ussy sat down and tried to keep himself from looking at the discarded parts of the armadillo. Why hadn't they been put in the garbage can? Where *was* the garbage can? Covertly Ussy looked around for it. He couldn't keep himself from looking at the dishes from which a meal had been eaten. The bits of food on them were dried—little, dark green strings of some kind of vegetable and blobs of congealed grits. The armadillo and the dishes shared the table with a basin of gray, used water, scummy on top.

Luke was delving into the sack of fruit and soap, laying out its contents. The bars and the box of soap only claimed his attention a second. He lifted an apple, polished it on his dirty shirt front and bit into it. Rejoicing in the taste of it, he talked around it. "Boy. I sure do like apples. You sure are good to us, Ussy. You know what I said to myself the first time I ever saw you?"

"What?" asked Ussy, not wanting to know.

"That you were a good guy. I knew you weren't like the others the first time I saw you and now it's been proved. My mother didn't thank you yet for buying her the ice but she will soon as she feels better. You know when a person's sick as she is they almost got to have ice."

His day's pay was in his right-hand pocket, deep down. Money was such a comforting thing to have. He wasn't going to give any more of his away. Packy or the people from the church or somebody was going to have to help the Wilders. He had done all he could do. He had his own canoe to paddle. "Luke," he said. "Luke, listen to me."

Luke had finished his apple. He tossed the core into the air and when it came down batted it with his foot. It rolled under the table.

"Luke, I've got an idea for you. You should listen to it."

Luke was choosing a banana from the little pile of fruit before him on the table. His hand wavered between one that was very yellow and another that had turned faintly brown. He selected the yellow one, peeled the skin back from it, stuck the tip of it in his mouth, bit down. "What?" he asked. "What idea?"

"It's about church."

"What church?"

"Do you go to one?"

"Huh-uh."

"Not ever?"

"Huh-uh. This is sure a good banana. You know the last time I had one? It was when we were in Georgia. I think it was Georgia. Yeh, Georgia. We were there working for a guy something like Packy. Mean. Big boss. You know how Packy talks. You want me to tell you something about Packy? He knows I'm not sixteen. Guys who're sixteen don't look like me. Do I look sixteen to you or thirteen?"

111

"Thirteen," answered Ussy and the feeling of helplessness in him was pulling. "But, Luke—"

"Well, to Packy I'm sixteen. I have to be else I couldn't work here. There's a law or something says you have got to be sixteen to work around tractors and big machinery. But anyway I was telling you about Georgia. We were up there picking cotton and pulling peanuts for this big, mean boss and one day I ate so many raw peanuts I got sick and somebody—I don't remember who—gave me a banana. It was a long time ago."

"Luke, I want to tell you about this idea I've got. See, when I went home yesterday I asked my sister if she didn't have some clothes she could give me for your mother. They're about the same size and I thought she could give me one of her dresses and a couple of other things. She said she gave all her old clothes to the church. She said you should join the church and they'd help you. Give you clothes and stuff."

Luke had finished the yellow banana. Delicately he wiped his fingers on his shirt. He eyed the brown banana. He glanced toward the bed against the wall. He lifted the brown banana and began peeling it. "I should save this one for my mother but she won't eat it. It'd just lay here and rot. You see how she is. She won't eat anything—"

"Luke, about the church—"

"What church?"

"My church."

"You go to church?"

"Sure."

"What for?"

"Well, to . . . well, all my family goes."

"What for?"

"We go because . . . we go because we believe in God." Ussy could feel his face start to redden. He wanted to get up and leave. He didn't like the way Luke was looking at him. He slid his hand into his pocket and felt his fifty-cent piece.

The second banana had disappeared into Luke's mouth. He wiped his hands on his hair this time. Being carefully pleasant and friendly he said, "Church is just one thing we've never taken up with. I went one time with a woman. That was when we lived in Colorado. They were having some kind of doings. I don't know the name of it but anyway they passed some little pieces of bread and some little glasses of grape juice only I didn't get any because I wasn't a member."

"It was communion," said Ussy and some imperfection in him loomed suddenly in the doorway of his mind. He couldn't talk to Luke about God or church. That was a preacher's job. If Luke didn't even know what church communion was he didn't know anything. It would be a big job, teaching him. Somebody would have to start at the beginning. A preacher, who knew how to explain things.

Luke was saying, "We don't need any clothes from any church. We got clothes. Wait, I'll show you." He skipped away from the table to a long, cardboard box at the far end of the room. He opened the box and began pulling articles of clothing from it: a long, full-

113

skirted red dress, very sheer with two white crinoline roses at its low V neckline, a brown satin jumper with tarnished buttons, a pair of tweed knickers with silver buckles at the knee-cuffs, an enormous, black, turtle-necked man's sweater. Luke held the sweater up to the light displaying its condition. "Ain't this something? I used it for a blanket last winter. Look how big it is. It's one hundred percent pure wool. The guy it used to belong to wore it when he went out to play golf on Saturdays. These holes in it don't bother anything. Just little old holes. Look at this one. I can't hardly get my fist through it, it's so small. Some church people gave us all this stuff. My mother's gonna wear that red dress to town when she gets over the malaria. I'm gonna wear this pair of knickers here. I won't need any shirt to go with 'em, because see? See how nice they come up to my neck? And my dad's going to wear this sweater. Won't we be the beauts though? Maybe we'll come to your church in these clothes. You think they'd let us in?"

"Our church wouldn't give you stuff like that," said Ussy stiffly. "They'd give you stuff you could use."

Luke dropped the red dress, the knickers, and the sweater back into the box. He rose and came back to the table. Solemn and regretful, he said, "Church people are funny. That's all I meant to say. They talk about God all the time. How much He loves everybody and is taking care of everybody—but us Wilders . . . well, when Marsh got adopted by those other people and they took him away . . . well, I asked God not to let it happen. It happened anyway. It was the onliest thing I ever asked Him for. He let it happen." Softly, Luke smiled. "I should tell you I don't have the watch I borrowed any more. I had to give it back and we don't have a clock. I don't know what time it is. The cook from the big house always goes to town about two o'clock. He said you should meet him at the rest-building. I told him we'd be waiting for him there."

He was released; he could go now. The rest of the afternoon was blessedly his. He didn't want Luke to go with him to the rest-building. "I can go alone," he said, edging toward the door. "I know the way. You'd better stay here and . . . and clean up. The box of soap I brought—it's good for anything. You can use it for everything; clothes, dishes, everything. Makes good suds."

"I'll try it tomorrow," said Luke. He wasn't interested in anything that cleaned. He was smiling his little, soft smile and he was determined to walk the long, hot trip to the rest-building with his friend. The determination showed in the way he carried himself out of the squalid little cabin and down the steps of it.

Ussy wanted to hurry. He was afraid it was already two o'clock; he had never been any good at judging the passage of time but Luke pointed to the position of the sun and said he thought it was only a little past one. They left the Wilder yard and cut back through the palmetto barren and Ussy lost his half-dollar.

Afterward he could not recollect how it happened. He had his hand out of his pocket and he had the half-dollar in the palm of it, sliding it back and forth and Luke, who was in back of him, said something to him—called his attention to something—and he turned and looked and turned back, going ahead again, and then his fifty-cent piece was gone. He rammed his hand deep in his pocket and felt for a hole but there was no hole. Had he put the coin back in his pocket? He stopped walking and turned around to face Luke. "I lost my half-dollar."

"What?" said Luke. "What?"

"My half-dollar. I had it a minute ago. I must've dropped it."

"I'd have seen you if you did that," said Luke. "It was silver, wasn't it?"

"Of course. It was a fifty-cent piece. You've seen them. They're all silver."

Luke was kneeling in the white sand of the scrub, picking up handfuls of the stuff, letting it sift between his fingers. There were several moments of confusion with both of them kneeling, running their hands through the hot sand, turning on their haunches to search with their eyes for a glint of metal. The wind rattled the stiff palmetto fronds and from afar there came a long, wild, lonely animal call.

"That's that panther I was telling you about," said Luke. He stood up and moved backward several feet, the waist-high palmettos closing around him. He shaded his eyes with one hand. "Did we come this way? It all looks the same to me. Now I can't remember . . . which way? . . . in all this sand you don't leave any tracks."

Ussy pivoted on his haunches and continued to

spread and sift the sand with his hands. "We came this way. It was right along here . . . no, maybe it was on back a little. Oh, zounds, I don't know. Aren't you going to help me look any more? What're you just standing there for?"

"Because I just know we aren't going to find it," answered Luke queerly indifferent. "We don't know if we came this way . . . I think it was over a little but anything lost in all this sand is just lost. Look at the way my foot sinks down in it. Look." He thrust his right leg forward and set his foot down and the loose, bleached sand closed around his shoe.

Ussy looked up to watch. He saw the sand spilling in on Luke's shoe and he saw Luke's leg with the material covering his thigh straining because of his position. He saw the round, hard outline beneath the material in Luke's pocket. Clarity came. He stood up. "Why, you've got my half-dollar! You picked it up when I dropped it! You've got it there in your pocket! I see it!"

"No," said Luke. "No." He pulled his leg back.

"Give it to me, Luke!"

"No! I haven't got it! This is something else in my pocket—"

"Show me!"

"You think I'm crazy? I wouldn't steal from you! I tell you I haven't got it! Stay away from me, Ussy! I don't wanta fight you! You're my friend! Ussy, stay away from me!"

Mad through and through, Ussy had reached Luke. Not ever a fighter, he lunged wildly at him. Luke

117

whirled away from him and attempted flight but the dense palmetto thicket hindered. He darted around a clump of the low, fan-leafed palms, attempted to hurdle another grouping of them and fell face down in the middle of them. The fruit of one, a half-inch-long black drupe, was wrenched from its stem in this scuffle. It fell to the back of his head and rolled downward to the waistband of his trousers. Two bees which had been attached to the drupe angrily buzzed. They joined wings and zoomed to Luke's ear. He screamed.

Ussy was on top of Luke, his legs and arms wrapped around Luke's torso and head and the sharp points of the spiny palmetto leaves were raking his face and arms. He plunged his hand into the thickness of Luke's greasy, filthy hair and yanked his head up. "Thief! Robber! Crook! Gimme my money! I want my money! Give it to me! You want me to kill you? I will! I want my money! Get up and give it to me!"

"Quit! Ow! Owwwww! Quit! You're breaking my back! Ewwwww! Quit!"

"You gonna give me my money? Are you?"

"I didn't know it was yours! I found it!"

"You knew it was mine! You saw me drop it! Didn't you? Didn't . . . you?"

"Yes! Quit! Lemme up!"

"You're nothing but a two-bit thief! I oughta kill you! Filth! Scum! You stink!"

"Ussy, you're . . . I can't breathe! Quit!"

"You gonna give me my money?"

"Yes! Yes! Lemme up!"

"Crook," panted Ussy and rolled off Luke's back to the ground. He was shaking and he couldn't stop this. His disgust for Luke and his contempt for him was thick and dirty in his belly and his throat and his mouth. It filled him to his lips and still more of it came. He looked down upon Luke lying in the palmettos. His ear where the bees had stung him was puffed out to the roundness of a tennis ball and he was sobbing.

"Just get up and give me my money," said Ussy coldly.

Luke stood. He came out of the palmettos, withdrew the half-dollar from his pocket and held it out to Ussy. "You beat me up," he said. "You shouldn't have done that. I'm smaller'n you. It wasn't fair."

Ussy pocketed his half-dollar. He stared at Luke. "What do you mean it wasn't fair? You stole my money—"

"I found it—"

"You knew it was mine. You saw me drop it. That's the same thing as stealing—"

"I thought you was my friend—"

"I am. I was. I brought you things to eat. I gave you money for ice and brought you the fruit and soap —"

"Soap," said Luke and the tears slid out of his eyes and down his cheeks. "Nobody can eat soap. You did that to make me feel bad."

"I did not! I did it because . . . well, you *need* soap. You need to wash yourself! You're filthy!"

Luke hung his head. "Nobody ever said that to me before. I thought you was my friend. I made a mistake, I guess. I guess I should say I'm sorry for making that mistake."

🪶 🪶 CHAPTER NINE

He was rid of Luke and Luke's problems and this was one of the best things he had ever experienced. It was an immense relief to be able to move to and from his job without the vexation of Luke; to have his mind free again. To be able to sleep again and be the hero in his dreams. In his mental life he chased around on a vehicle that was half horse and half motorcycle. It drank gasoline and ate corn and could scale a wall three stories high and jump over raging rivers. His speciality was rescuing people. His dreams made him laugh, they were so impossible and silly.

In his spare time Ussy hung around Medina's Motorcycle Shop, gawking at the new and used models. They simply cost too much and one day he ruthlessly abandoned his idea to buy one. When the time came he'd hitchhike his way out of Medina to San Francisco.

At the end of every working day he counted his growing hoard of money. He never spent a nickel of it. A horror movie named the *The Clutching Hand* came to Medina and Winnie coyly suggested that he loosen up and take her and Veronica Lovejoy to see it. "Nothing doing," he said. "If you and Veronica want to see *The Clutching Hand* go out and get yourself a job. That's what I had to do. I don't know what you women think anyway. That men are just here to support you?"

Trying to coax him, Winnie said, "Veronica is in love with you. If you can imagine such a thing. She says she's going to marry you. You could do a lot worse, Uss. Veronica has lovely manners and she's smart, too. You'd better be thinking about it, Uss, and not burn any bridges behind you."

"Marriage is for the buzzards," declared Ussy who, on this Saturday morning was rigging up a contraption which would haul fireplace wood from the woodpile to the back porch. Come the winter he wouldn't be here to perform this chore and he wanted it to be made easier for those he would leave behind.

From a junk yard he had got two pulleys and had nailed one of these to an outside wall of the back porch. Through the grooved rims of the pulleys he threaded a length of flexible clothesline, hammering the two tied ends together so that the knot would pass through the rims and would present no obstruction. To the pulley line he attached a piece of stout rope with a slipknot in the loose end of it big enough to go around a small log or several pieces of wood. To test his invention (with Winnie looking on) he carried a small log from the woodpile, knelt in the yard beside the dangling piece of rope, placed the log in the slipknot, skipped back to the porch, and applied pulling force to the line. It worked. The small log in the slipknot, dangling about a foot from the ground, traveled smoothly toward the back porch steps.

"Aha, she cried as she cracked her wooden leg," said Ussy and sat down to rest.

"I can see everybody in the United States buying one," said Winnie. "Are you going to patent it?"

"Patent it?"

"It's an invention," said Winnie. "When you invent something you're supposed to write to Washington, D. C., and tell them about it. If it's a good idea and nobody else has thought of it first they'll give you a paper with a number on it. That's what a patent is. All inventions are patented. You going to write to Washington about your invention?"

"I hadn't thought about it," replied Ussy and took a breath to expand his chest muscles. "I might. It's a good invention. Nobody likes to carry wood in from a woodpile, especially when it's cold or raining."

"Yes," agreed Winnie. "I'll bet a lot of people would like to have one of those. The only thing is, won't it take two people to work it? What I mean is, now it only takes one person to carry wood in from the woodpile; he just walks out, picks it up and carries it in. But this invention of yours now . . . I think it will take two people. One to go out to the woodpile and carry the log or the pieces of wood over to that piece of rope there and put it inside the knot and one to stand on the porch and work the pulleys. Or else if you think only one should work it he could go out to the woodpile, get the pieces of wood or the log, carry it to the rope, put it inside the loop and then come back to the porch and pull it in. Yes, one person could work your invention, Uss."

She was such a loudmouth. So know-it-all. Such a female.

He couldn't think of any way to correct the engineering flaw in his invention and this failure irked him. He felt the need to talk with somebody above the level of his own intelligence and went to spend the afternoon with Mr. Suffrin who had experienced a failure of his own. The coat to his new pin-striped suit hugged his chest so tightly that it couldn't be buttoned and the sleeves didn't match; one hung down to the middle of his hand while the other was above his wrist. "Which just goes to show you," said Mr. Suffrin, "that even a man like Pasquale knows what he's talking about sometimes. As soon as I can get up enough nerve I'll take this mess to him and see if he can straighten it out."

Mr. Suffrin had a stamp collection which his father had started for him when he was twelve years old. It was contained in a big, leather-bound album which Mr. Suffrin handled lovingly. "With some people the collecting of postage stamps is something of a mania," he said, turning the album leaves to show Ussy the little printed squares which were affixed to the pages on hinges. "No one can say for certain just when stamp collecting began but I like the story about a frivolous young lady in London, back in 1841, who wanted to cover the walls of her bedroom with cancelled postage stamps so she advertised in a newspaper and people sent them to her. The story goes that she succeeded in collecting sixteen thousand stamps."

With his head bent into the album Ussy gazed admiringly at a little black picture of Andrew Jackson, seventh President of the United States. "I always liked Andrew Jackson. So strong. He wasn't always running around asking other people to help him make up his mind about things. I just can't stand people who always have to lean on somebody else."

"Here's an interesting stamp," said Mr. Suffrin, pointing with a pair of tweezers to a little scarlet square. "This is a 1928 Valley Forge Issue. Someday it might be worth a lot of money."

"Interesting," said Ussy. "But I like the ones with Presidents on them better. It takes a lot of nerve to be President of the United States. Presidents have to be strong. Weak people make me sick, the way they always hang on other people."

Mr. Suffrin glanced at him over the top of his spectacles. "We've had some weak Presidents, Ussy. They're only human; they're just men."

"Andrew Jackson," said Ussy, going back to the postage picture of the seventh President, "looked a little bit like a guy I know. His name is Luke Wilder and he's a pain in the whatzis. I think I'm rid of him now but he always used to hang on me wanting something. I got to the point where I hated him. He's filthy. I took him some soap but he wouldn't even wash himself. I just can't stand anybody who has to depend on somebody else for every little thing, can you?"

Mr. Suffrin was turning the leaves of his album, giving half of his attention to his stamps. In a minute, in a practical voice he said, "I'm not crazy about them but at the same time I recognize the fact that not everybody is as independent as I am. This world is full of two kinds of people, Ussy. The leaners and the leaned-upon."

"Luke Wilder is a leaner," declared Ussy. "He's worthless. He's a rat."

Solemn and pleasant, Mr. Suffrin closed the stamp album. He leaned back in his chair and with no show of teacher-authority in his voice said, "But you're sorry for him."

"I was," confessed Ussy. "But not any more. He tried to steal some money from me and I got rid of him."

Mr. Suffrin smiled. "You want a little sermon, Ussy? No, I can see you don't but I'll give you one anyway. I didn't write it. A novelist by the name of William Makepeace Thackeray did. He said, 'Dependence is a perpetual call upon humanity, and a greater incitement to tenderness and pity than any other motive whatever.' "

Ussy bit his knuckles. "Zounds," he said.

125

"It's simple when you break it down, Ussy. Perpetual means forever and incitement means to arouse. So here you have Mr. Thackeray telling us that forever we can look forward to having somebody around like your pain in the whatzis—your Luke Wilder. And then he goes on to suggest that when we see them we won't be able to stop ourselves from feeling tenderness and pity."

"If that guy William What's-His-Face Thackeray thinks I'm supposed to go around feeling tender and sorry for somebody like Luke Wilder forever he'd better think again," said Ussy.

"William Makepeace Thackeray is dead," said Mr. Suffrin. "He died in 1863 so when you speak of him it should be in the past tense. And he didn't say you were *supposed* to go around feeling sorry for people like Luke Wilder. He said you would in spite of yourself. Because you are stronger than Luke Wilder. You have more and know more."

"Luke Wilder is a viper and a low-down rat," said Ussy. "I never did feel tender toward him and I'm through being sorry for him. I tried to help him and it didn't do one bit of good."

"Then let's not talk about him any more," said Mr. Suffrin. And said how about a cup of good, strong tea.

On his job Ussy still saw Luke and his father but he avoided any contact with them; when he saw either of them coming he turned his back or walked away. They were such no-good people. Luke didn't do any-

126

thing about his dirtiness and Luke's father . . . well, he was just plain sorry. He claimed to be a truck driver but every day he and Packy had arguments about his shortcomings as one. Luke's father had some pretty rough habits. He chewed tobacco and the juice from his plug was always around his mouth. He was always scratching himself and yawning, showing his vacant mouth, and his sullen hatred of Packy was always there, just underneath the surface of him. Packy was Mr. Wilder's enemy. The vegetables he had to haul from the fields and the heat—these also were Mr. Wilder's enemies. When Packy wasn't around he swore at the heat and his job and tried to boss the boys from Medina: "You all're supposed to tote your own crates to the end of the rows when you get 'em filled. You're the ones reapin' all the benefits from this project, not me. Ary another one o' you sets another one of his crates down in the middle of a row like this it'll just stay there, you hear me? I'm an old man and I'm sick. If you had any respect for age you'd show me a little like you're supposed t'do. A couple of you boys get over here and help me load up this truck. Move now. I ain't got all day."

The boys from Median hardly ever obeyed any of Mr. Wilder's orders. They held their noses when he came close to them. They laughed like hyenas at his mistakes and when he and Packy argued they abandoned their work to sit and silently, expectantly watch. They wanted to see Packy lose his temper completely and use violence against Mr. Wilder. Packy was twice Mr. Wilder's size and knew how to box. At college one time he had knocked a guy out in the first round. Mr. Wilder wouldn't be any match at all for Packy.

The boys of the Medina Summer Work Camp— there were only four left now—knelt between their rows of vegetables and pulled and whacked and watched. They were bored and they wanted their boredom relieved and so this watching of theirs became a game. How long would it be before Packy took a poke at Mr. Wilder? Or would Mr. Wilder be the one to take the first poke? Maybe, if the fight was a good enough one, Mr. Wilder might get himself killed. Dirty old dingbat. They'd all be witnesses to the fight. They'd all have to go to court and swear to what they had witnessed. It would be kind of interesting to be a court witness. Sammy Hicks had been one once. Late one night a burglar had broken into the house next door to his and Sammy had been the only witness. He had gone to court and been a star witness. He had positively identified the burglar. Now the criminal was serving time on the chain gang.

To Ussy this story of Sammy's was drivel, not even worthy of the scantest attention. He resented Sammy's taking up his time with it. He had work to do —money to earn—and Sammy got in his way. Days before, the sun had passed its summer solstice—it was now at its farthest point from the equator and in its southward motion it appeared to be standing still. The forepart of the days was very hot and dry but in the afternoons the clouds would begin to bank and turn dark and then it would rain and then the earth would steam. The tomatoes on the maudlin green vines in the truck fields were ripe and overripe and now it was important to harvest them as quickly as possible and to keep at it. It was important to Ussy not to be hindered by the silly prattle of the others. He couldn't laugh at Sammy's dirty jokes. He had never heard a funny dirty joke.

"It's because you don't listen," said Sammy and his red lips curved softly against his white teeth. "Let me tell it to you again."

"Get out of my way," said Ussy. "I don't want to hear your old, dumb dirty joke."

Sammy plucked a fat, ripe tomato from the vine nearest him. With his thumbnail he lacerated the soft, waxen skin of it and a little of its juice spurted out over his fist. He opened his hand and with a little, wet *plop* the ruined tomato fell to the ground. He took a handkerchief from his pocket and wiped his hands. He smiled his slow, sweet smile. "Excuse me," he said. "I forgot I was talking to you. I forgot there are some people who don't think anything's funny. What are you working so hard for?"

"Because that's what I'm here to do. How about moving out of my row, Sammy? You're in my way."

"Oh, excuse me," said Sammy and stood up. He started to move away but then turned and came back. "Now I remember what I came down here to ask you," he said. "It's about your friend. That Wilder kid. Nobody's seen him around today. Where is he?"

"I don't know, Sammy."

"His father says he's sick."

"Then maybe he's sick, Sammy."

"I don't think he's sick."

"Don't you, Sammy?"

"Yesterday when we were leaving I saw him down near the road. He was lying in the bushes asleep."

"Well, maybe he was sleepy, Sammy."

"Aren't you his friend any more?"

"No."

"Why?"

"None of your beeswax, Sammy."

"He's trash," said Sammy and walked away to his own row and the others came from theirs and gathered around him and he told them a joke and their communal laughter was light and bright.

It was a little past two o'clock in the afternoon of this day. Packy was absent from the work in the fields. He had gone to the big house to nurse an ailing wisdom tooth. It was a little early for the daily weather change but out over the gallberry flats and the palmetto barrens the clouds had begun to amass and behind these, as they slowly piled and darkened, cracks of lightning occasionally sizzled. Thunder, faint and distant, sounded and the wind began to liven, bending the tops of the tall, spindly pines that ringed the truck gardens. Soon it would rain.

Across the fields, bouncing and jogging in the truck he never seemed quite able to control, there came Mr. Wilder and Luke was with him. Ussy looked up from his tomato vines and saw the faces of the Wilders, dirty and sullen through the wavy windshield of the truck. Mr. Wilder was driving fast—too fast—not driving parallel with the irrigation furrows running between the crop rows but going across them. There was recklessness in this and defiance, for the farm's irrigation system was Packy's and hadn't he made it understood to Mr. Wilder that the furrows were for water and that he wasn't to drive his truck in them or across them?

Mr. Wilder wasn't caring. He was driving across the irrigation ditches. The back end of his truck contained piled, empty vegetable crates and these were being bounced around and the anger of Mr. Wilder showed in the way he was wrenching the steering wheel of the truck first to the left and then to the right senselessly and the rain was coming. The gunmetal clouds in the west were being blown clear of the skyline. The wind was lifting them and they were moving in a ragged line over the gallberry flats and the palmetto barrens toward the truck farm.

The boys from Medina had a total of eight crates of tomatoes waiting for Mr. Wilder. They had been cooperative and had placed these all together at the end of one row. They didn't care if the rain was coming. Packy wasn't there to order them to the rest-building so they were unbuttoning their shirts and lifting their faces to the sky, waiting for the first wet drops to fall. They were going to enjoy this piece of fun. Sammy Hicks had taken off all his clothes except his tight undershorts. He was prancing up and down, showing off to the others and they were grinning at him and being encouraged to strip to their own underwear and Mr. Wilder was coming fast across the irrigation ditches, the thickset truck dangerously lurching.

It reached the spot where the eight full tomato crates waited. It slammed into them. It went through them and pieces of the smashed crates and red fruit flew. Luke screamed something to his father and the truck, now halfway down Ussy's row, came to an abrupt stop.

All in one instant the clouds, which now were directly overhead, opened, the rain fell in a gray flood and from nowhere Packy was there, jerking the door of the truck open, pulling Mr. Wilder from it, yelling at the older man and beating him on the face with his fists. "Lame-brain! Stupid! Good-for-nothing stupid! I saw you, the way you were driving! This wasn't any accident! I saw the whole thing! What's the matter with you? You crazy?"

Mr. Wilder was trying to get his arms up to his face to shield it. His mouth was open and he was gulping air. His frail legs nimbly carried him backward out of the range of Packy's blows. "Packy . . . Packy . . . watch out now! Who you're beatin' on! They's a law! The law'll be on my side if you hurt me!"

The rain was between Packy and Mr. Wilder and Mr. Wilder was running around to the back end of the truck and Packy was running after him. The boys from Medina were yelling encouragement to Packy: "Get him, Packy! He did it on purpose! He ruined eight crates of your tomatoes on purpose! We saw him! We'll be your witness!"

And Luke was coming out of his side of the truck's cab. "Dad! Dad! He's bigger'n you are! Don't fight him! Run!"

Ussy saw Mr. Wilder reach for something in the

back end of the truck. It was a short-handled pitchfork. Ussy saw the weapon in Mr. Wilder's wet hands and he saw Packy reach through the slats of the rear end of the truck for his own weapon, a spoon-shaped spade. Packy pulled the spade out from between the slats and Mr. Wilder, the pitchfork balanced in his hands, waited. The boys from Medina weren't saying anything now. They had drawn together, all but Ussy who still stood beside the stripped tomato plants in his row.

Some of the rain was turning to hail, big, white pellets bouncing from the hood of the truck and its top. The hail was in Ussy's hair and there were pieces of it sliding cold down his neck and arms and it was on the wet ground before him bouncing and the sound of this weather was blocking out hearing but through the gray rain and the falling, white ice he could see the murderous intent in Packy's face and out of the corner of his eye he could see Luke who had run forward toward his father and then stopped.

Ussy saw Luke's fright plastered big and white and all in one terrible instant, awareness and understanding of the Wilders and things concerning the Wilders was upon him, inside him, expanding.

Packy had the spade in his hands and Mr. Wilder had the pitchfork in his and they were watching each other through the rain and hail and in a second now one of them would move.

Something punched at Ussy's insides. He opened his mouth and screamed. "Packy, don't! Don't! He doesn't know . . . You've got more and you know more than he does, Packy! You're stronger and smarter! Mr. Suffrin . . . my history teacher says . . . Packy!"

Neither Packy nor Mr. Wilder was paying attention to him. Packy was moving toward his migrant employee and raising his shovel. Mr. Wilder's face, grayer than the gray rain, showed his awful hatred of Packy. He raised his pitchfork, aimed it at Packy's abdomen and ran forward.

CHAPTER TEN

Packy didn't die from the wounds inflicted on him by Mr. Wilder. He lay in a room in Medina's little hospital and in a few days he began to heal and was able to sit up and receive nourishment. His sympathizers sent flowers and get-well cards.

Mr. Wilder was taken to jail and it was said of him that he cursed until the air around him turned blue. He refused to say he was sorry. "I was only protecting myself," he said. "Packy would have killed me if I hadn't laid him out first. Go and ask the boys that were workin' there that day if that's not the truth. Make 'em swear to tell the truth then you'll find out what it is. Maybe you will. If you don't find out the truth . . . well, then I guess the state of Florida will just have to take care of me the rest of my life."

Ussy tried to justify Mr. Wilder's crime to his father. "Pop, it wasn't Mr. Wilder's fault. Packy started the fight. Even before Mr. Wilder could get out of his truck Packy started to beat on him with his fists."

"The other boys don't say that, Ussy. They say Mr. Wilder started it."

"They're lying, Pop. Honest."

"Ussy, I'm so tired of hearing about it. Every night—"

"Pop, I am, too. I'm tired talking about it. But don't you understand? It's not just the lie I'm talking about. It's the other."

"What other, Ussy?"

"But I told you! Weren't you listening? Pop, the important thing is. . . . the most important thing is that Packy knows more than people like Mr. Wilder. He's been to college and studied things so he knows more and he has more and so it's his place to watch out for people like Mr. Wilder."

"Ussy, who told you that?"

"Nobody. I guess it was Mr. Suffrin. I was telling him about the Wilders and he said dependence was a perpetual call upon humanity."

"Oh, Ussy."

"Pop, the Wilders don't even know enough to keep themselves clean and Luke doesn't even know what church communion is and . . . and they gave one of their children away."

"Ussy, I want you to stop worrying about this. There is going to be a trial and then the judge will decide what will happen to Mr. Wilder. Please let me read my paper. Please let me have a little peace when I come home at night."

He had bungled in his attempt to present his case for the Wilders to his father. He could not present his picture of the migrant family clearly enough to make anyone understand the true fault of them.

The awful truth was that there was some knowledge of the Wilders not clear even to himself. Somewhere way back in their beginnings something had gone wrong and now the awful truth was that they were beat to the bone and it wasn't enough to say that other people who knew more and had more should watch out for them.

There was a thing remembered about Luke which kept pulling at Ussy—the porch plants in their rusty cans on the broken-down porch of the dingy migrant cabin on the Snyder farm. Anybody who cared enough about a bunch of little stringy plants to lug them all the way from Colorado . . . well, there had to be something to him besides just filth and low-downness. There had to be something promising beneath the dirt and pettiness. The awful truth of the matter was that before he could resume his own plans and life he had to do something about Luke. It was a necessity.

Awake at three o'clock in the morning, Ussy worried about the Wilders. Luke and his mother were going to have to vacate the cabin on the Snyder farm and find a place in town. They had no money and no friends. Their provider sat in jail waiting for his trial. Who would help them?

Ussy closed his eyes. All these troubles at this hour of the night. They weren't his and yet until he did something about them they would be with him. There had to be something wrong with him. To be awake here at three o'clock in the morning worrying about people he hardly knew. He detested the Wilders.

He couldn't shake the worry. The next day Ussy went to town on some private errands and from there he hitchhiked a ride out to the Snyder farm and walked from the big, main house to the cabin in the woods. Luke did not act glad to see him. The two boys sat in the hot, ugly, one-room house and Luke's mother lay without moving or speaking on the bed against the wall and there was another dead armadillo, this one still in its shell, lying on the floor beneath the table.

Ussy asked, "Aren't you going to eat him?"

Childishly sullen, Luke disclosed a sour secret. "My mother's going to have another baby. It wasn't malaria any of the time. I am trying to think. I am wondering what I can do. I can't stay here with another baby coming. I don't have anything to eat. I can't live on armadillos. Besides some tomatoes that's all we've had to eat for four days. I'm a little scared. I heard the panther last night. Up close. Some night he might just get in here and kill me." Luke hung his head. "We got to be out of here by tomorrow. I asked my mother where to go but she don't know. She won't talk to me. She don't care."

He had come to make two suggestions. There was a furnished room up over Pepper's Pool Hall in Medina and there was a job in the pool hall itself. Under much questioning and persuasion Mr. Pepper had admitted that he could use the services of a young man for all-around work. He would pay Luke eight dollars a week to start.

There remained the question of what the Wilders could eat until the first paycheck. Ussy had five dollars in his pocket. To part with them would be a terrible wrench. It was part of his cache of getaway money. To gain peace and freedom for himself he might have to part with them. . . .

Ussy said, "Luke, I've got a couple of ideas for you."

Luke was walking around the room kicking at things, punching them with his fists and feet, mad at them. He avoided the corner containing the bed. He yanked at the clothes hanging on the wall pegs and a dress with torn sleeves and a dirt-splotched front fell shapelessly to the floor. He went to the box containing the cast-off clothing the Wilders would never use and stood over it shaking his head. "I think my dad'll go to prison. They're saying he will. I went to see him and he said he didn't care. It's the truth. He don't care what happens to us. They told us we got to move on, where to I don't know. I showed you the clothes here in this box. People give them to us and they tell us to move on. What we supposed to do? Go live under a tree? I can't live under no tree. I don't even have a tree. If

I asked somebody to live under their tree they'd tell me to move on."

The dead armadillo so close to Ussy's foot smelled. He turned in his chair and saw the basin of soiled water on the end of the table and the unwashed dishes. The box of soap he had brought days and days ago lay unopened on its side beneath the table. There was all the dirt and slovenliness. He wanted to get up and run away from this and he could not.

"Luke," said Ussy. "There's a room up over the pool hall in Medina that's for rent. It's two dollars and a half a week. You can move there. It's not much but it's clean. It's got a little oil stove to cook on and two beds and there's a bathroom down the hall. I went by to see Mr. Pepper just before I came out here. He'll rent you the room and he'll give you a job. He owns the pool hall."

With both hands Luke was rubbing his pinched face. "A job in a pool hall. Well, that would be all right, I guess. But I got to figure out . . . there's all this stuff I'll have to move. I guess if we can get it all loaded in the truck my mother could get up long enough to drive us. My dad never taught me how to drive. Or any of my brothers."

Mrs. Wilder was awake and sitting up. Her face was sallow and gaunt. Dull and remote, she sat in a humped attitude of supplication. Probably even in her beginning she had never been bright and assertive. Probably she had never tried to control what happened to her. There was a loose, faraway look in her eyes. She pushed at her tan hair and it slipped through

140

her fingers and fell again, straight around her face and shoulders. "I wisht I had some ice," she said. "It's so hot and I feel so bad. Luke, maybe you could go up to the big house and ask them for a little piece of ice for me? Just a little piece?"

Luke went to stand before his mother. "Ma, I can't go to the big house and ask for anything. We got to load up our things and move now. Ussy has come to help us. You'll have to get up and drive us. You can do that, can't you?"

"Sure," replied Luke's mother and lay back down.

"The truck's out back, Ma. You'll have to get up and bring it around to the front."

"Oh," said Luke's mother and like a sleepwalker rose and left the cabin by the rear door. She brought the truck around to the front of the house and sat in the cab of it, head back and eyes closed.

"She says she's always like this when she's going to have a baby," said Luke. "It don't make sense. She's sick enough to die for about two months but then she gets all right. I'm glad I'm not a woman." He was pulling the clothes down from the wall pegs, making a haphazard pile of them on the floor. "We won't pack any of this stuff. We aren't going very far and anyway we don't have any suitcases. You can take this pile out, Ussy. Just throw it in the back of the truck."

He hadn't thought to physically help with the job of moving the Wilders. He had business of his own to worry about. But how could he refuse?

They worked for over an hour emptying the cabin of the Wilder possessions. Luke wouldn't leave even the most worthless. There was an electric iron without a handle, a radio case without insides, a cigar box containing an assortment of rusted nails and screws, one wooden candlestick, a cloth bag of old buttons and pieces of string.

"What about the armadillo?" asked Ussy.

Luke gave the dead animal his beady attention. "It's spoiled, I think. It might make us sick to eat it. I don't know though. It's all we got. We don't have no money for food. Unless I can borrow some from somebody. That Mr. Pepper at the pool hall is gonna trust me for the rent, ain't he?"

It was a wrench as Ussy had known it would be—to take his five dollars from his pocket and hand it to Luke.

"I'll give it back to you as soon as I get my first pay," said Luke. He was excited and happy, giddy with relief and good humor. On the way in to Medina he made plans and promises. "The first time I get paid I'm gonna buy some steak. A lot of it. I'm going to buy me some pants and a shirt, too. I'm so tired of wearing other people's clothes. I'll work hard at this job you got for me. That Mr. Pepper won't be sorry he hired me. Me and him will be friends. Hey, you know what I'd like to do right now?"

"What?" asked Ussy, cramped tight between Mrs. Wilder and Luke in the cab of the truck.

"Go swimming," said Luke. "Did somebody tell me there was a place to go swimming in Medina?"

"There's Mullet River," said Ussy. "But it isn't in Medina."

The close, dry heat in the cab of the truck was making him a little sick. There was that and there was the odor of the Wilders, thick in his nose. He tried to steer his attention away from these immediate disagreements and think of pleasant things. Something was happening to his escape-dream. It was getting harder and harder to summon the early, bright thoughts of it to mind. There were too many other things interfering. It sure was a fact that dependence was a perpetual call upon humanity. His answer to the call had taken another five dollars of his money and now, because the Medina Work Camp for Boys was finished, he was without a job. He had to get another one right away; maybe he could find two. One for during the regular workday and one for the evenings. Jobs were scarcer than hens' teeth but nothing was insurmountable.

CHAPTER ELEVEN

Ussy went out and scoured the town and found two, part-time jobs. Soon, because of the energies he expended on them, he was lean to the point of being bareboned. His stomach manufactured all the right properties from the food he shoveled into it but his frame became weedier than it had ever been.

At three o'clock each morning he popped from his bed and by three fifteen was standing at the curb in front of his house waiting for the truck from the Sunshine Dairy. The driver, who had suffered a swimming accident and who now wore a brace on his neck, drove through the sleeping neighborhoods of Medina, up and down and around and through the night-cooled streets. He stopped at each customer's house and Ussy, standing ready with the bottles of milk and cream and the cartons of eggs and butter, would jump from the truck and run. Notes in the empty bottles in the doorways usually meant two trips. Dogs lay in wait for him. They snarled at him, barked at him, and chased him. He had promised speed and he fulfilled the promise. He spoke to the dogs or kicked out at them and ran through the wet grass, up the steps of the houses and down. The dairy truck always worked a little ahead of him, inching forward to the next house, a white blur in the murky street. He became an athlete.

About three quarters of the way through the deliveries day would break, come shining red and yellow through the trees, climbing up to the tops of them and over, flushing the sky with day color.

At seven or thereabouts he was finished with this job for the day. He went home and slept until lunchtime. At one P.M. he went to the office of the *Medina Herald.* He had convinced Mr. George, the publisher and editor of the *Herald* that he wanted to become a newspaperman so for the sum of four dollars a week he was allowed to sweep, wash windows, clean the rest room, take telephone messages when Mr. George was out, watch the printing machine, and deliver hand-bills. The *Herald* leaned heavily on the business of handbill printing. For an extra amount Mr. George would plaster them all over town. He said there was money in the grocery business. "But I think it's duller than dishwater," he said.

"Groceries just don't interest me," commented Ussy.

"I'm the kind of guy who's just got to get out and see things," said Mr. George.

"Me, too," said Ussy.

"When are you going and how far?" inquired Mr. George.

Wondering if Mr. George was the kind of person who could keep a secret, Ussy looked away from him. "I didn't say I was going anywhere."

"When I was your age," said Mr. George, "I was always running away. Of course they always found me and brought me back but that was one of the most interesting times of my life. One time I got as far as Kansas. They grow a lot of wheat in Kansas. You ever see a wheat field?"

"No," answered Ussy. "But I want to. I want to see everything."

"Oh, I did, too," said Mr. George. "But if I had it to do over again I think I'd plan things a little better. There are a lot of people out there and not all of them are friendly."

Ussy bit his knuckles. His dream of going to San Francisco was so tired. After a minute he said, "I had my plans all made but then I had to help somebody."

"Well," said Mr. George. "That's the way with plans. Sometimes even the best laid ones don't work out. But you've got lots of time; you've got your whole life ahead of you. How about getting a move on? I

146

promised the Piggly-Wiggly to get these handbills out this afternoon. You see all the good bargains they got beginning tomorrow?"

"I'm not much interested in grocery bargains," said Ussy.

"Don't skip anybody," said Mr. George. "You can take this pile and start with the stores and businesses. You should run out about the time you hit Center Street. You can phone me from somebody's house and I'll hop in my car and bring you some more."

With the long, slick handbills draped over his left arm Ussy left the office of the *Herald* and went out into the streets. He delivered the handbills. At Delphine's Cafe he handed one to each coffee-drinking customer and two to Delphine. At the Medina State Bank he distributed six.

Wanting to avoid Luke Wilder as he had been doing for two weeks now, he started past Pepper's Pool Hall but didn't make it. Luke, resplendently attired, appeared suddenly in the wide, open-air doorway. He wore a zoot suit, burnt-orange in color. It had a draped jacket with heavily padded shoulders, flared lapels, and a row of pearl buttons on each sleeve. Its high-waisted trousers were sharply pleated and had full legs which tapered to narrow cuffs. Luke wore a pale green shirt and a satin-finished tie which was emerald green. He wore orange shoes, brilliantly polished, with pointed toes. Grinning, he came out onto the sidewalk and joined Ussy. "I was hoping to see you. Where you going so fast?"

Ussy shifted his load of handbills from his left arm

to his right. "I'm working. Delivering these hand-bills."

Luke knelt and with the palm of his hand polished the tips of the hideous orange shoes. His dark hair looked as if it had just been washed; it was loose and shiny. Awkwardly graceful, childishly ridiculous in his awful clothes, embarrassed, brash, he stood up. "I'm glad you came along. I started to come to your house last night but then I thought you wouldn't want to see me. Ussy, Mr. Pepper fired me. I don't have a job now."

Ussy looked at Luke. He wanted to run. He transferred the handbills back to his left arm. He stood and waited for Luke's confidence.

"I don't know if you remember my plants," said Luke. "The ones I brought from Colorado. But anyway, yesterday I set them on the windowsill of our room up over this place because they've got to have air and sun only it wasn't wide enough because the screen was in between. So I took the screen out and by accident I dropped one of my plants on Mr. Pepper. He was in the alley out back cleaning up some trash."

"And now he's in the hospital," said Ussy, fancying the worst.

"No. But he had to go to a doctor and get a couple of stitches taken in his head. When he came back he was so mad he fired me. He told us to move."

"You should have been more careful," said Ussy. "You'll know better next time. Luke, I've got to go now."

"I've already got us another place," said Luke,

pressing his explanation. "It's in a big house with lots of other roomers. The lady that owns it is nice; she likes me. I helped her fix one of her doors that was stuck. She's going to trust me for our rent until I can get another job but in between I need a little money. For food for my mother and me. Ussy, could you lend me some money? Five or six dollars? I'll pay you back. Honest. Just as soon as I get another job I'll pay you back."

Standing there in the hot sun feeling the weight of the handbills on his arm and feeling the weight of Luke—the now familiar feeling of strange helplessness pulling—Ussy sought to toughen himself against the demand confronting him. "Luke," he said, "I can't. I've got my own stuff to think about. There's something I want to do and it's going to take all the money I've got."

Abruptly the money seemed to become an unimportant issue with Luke. He came two steps toward Ussy and stopped. He lowered his head and began a critical survey of the way he was dressed. "A guy like me," he said, "always has to learn everything the hard way. Somebody always has to show us how to do and be because we haven't got sense enough to know ourselves. I look like a monkey in these clothes, don't I?"

"They're just clothes," said Ussy.

"I hate 'em," said Luke and his features began to separate in the oddest way. The expression in his eyes began to burn angrily and color, red as rouge, spread across his cheeks yet his mouth was cold and steady. "I ought to take them back to the guy that sold 'em to

149

me and punch him in the face. I told him I just wanted plain stuff like what you wear. I asked him if he knew you and he said yes and I told him I wanted to be like you and wear the kind of clothes you wear and he said he knew what I meant. But then . . . Well, I don't know. I guess it was my own fault. I guess I just got carried away. I forgot to remember that you wouldn't wear stuff like this. I look like an ape in them, don't I?"

Something very unsettling was touching the very foundation of Ussy. In the most startling way he had a sudden feeling of floating. To his knowledge, not ever before in all of his life, had he influenced anybody. He hadn't known that he possessed this power, yet apparently he did because here was another human being who had just said so. He meant it, too, and that was the strangest part. That he was being honest about it showed in Luke's face. Ussy squinted his eyes and peered at Luke and tried to detect trickery in his face but there was none.

Far away in the marshy distance the limpkins were calling and above the town of Medina the sun was brighter than it had ever been. Ussy raised his free hand to his mouth and bit his knuckles. He couldn't answer Luke's question because it was forgotten. He couldn't speak because his tongue wouldn't move.

Luke was removing the coat to his suit. He folded it carefully and laid it on the sidewalk. Next he removed his tie and laid that on top of the coat. "It makes me so mad," he said. "I get so mad at the things I do. I'm not dopey. I can do things as good as anybody else—you, for instance. But I'm always doing the wrong things. I've always got to have somebody show me how to do and be."

Despising his helplessness, Ussy knew what he was going to do. In just a second now he knew he was going to hand over to Luke what money there was in his pocket and he knew that this would reduce to a shred his getaway dream.

The wind that was whiffing around through the downtown streets of Medina that day riffled the hand-bills on Ussy's arm. For some reason the passing motion of it left him giddy.

Ussy put his hand in his pocket.

CHAPTER TWELVE

There was a short period of feeling extremely virtuous. His sacrifice had been a noble thing and he was proud to have made it. For several days he felt good and generous about it but then there came a change and it was as if he had suffered a grave illness. Recuperating, he sat wanly on the front porch of his home reading the newspaper. He observed the comings and goings of his family like a sick person watches and he forgave them everything. Like himself they were victims of their own affairs and only trying to make the best of it.

He gave up both of his jobs and spent many long, aimless hours just wandering around through the neighborhoods of the town, spying disinterestedly on the people in the houses. They spoke to him from their doorways and porches and he said, "Hey," and shuffled past. That they didn't run out and tell him they were going to the Congo to hunt elephants or yell to him that there was a mad dog on the loose and for him to run for the sheriff wasn't at all an angering thing any more. They were just people who liked things nice and quiet.

He lifted his feet and moved past their houses. It gave him a twinge to see the older ones so busy in their little tinkering duties. Someday he himself would be a little, baggy, old man trotting around with a watering can.

One day in his wanderings Ussy found a long stick and pretended he was blind. With his eyes closed, he held the stick in front of him, tapping it the way a blind person does, and didn't direct his feet. He didn't know where he was headed until he stood in front of Mr. Suffrin's ramshackle gate. Quietly astonished he opened his eyes and surveyed Mr. Suffrin's willy-nilly yard. The eggplants and butter beans had grown at least another inch. The marigolds had recently been watered; their leaves sparkled in the sun. Ussy pushed Mr. Suffrin's gate open and went up the walk. He mounted the steps and called and his teacher came to the door.

Mr. Suffrin had a new hobby; he was building a model ship. He had sent away for the building kit and when completed the ship would be thirty-six inches long and twenty-two inches high.

"This is a model of one of the first Yankee Clippers ever built," said Mr. Suffrin. "In her day she was the fastest thing on the water and the most graceful. Men fell in love with her, she was so beautiful. They wrote sonnets and poetry to her."

"It'll be nice," said Ussy.

Mr. Suffrin sat cross-legged on the floor with tools and the contents of the kit spread out all around him. He held a block of wood in his lap and consulted the book of instructions. "Let's see now. Ah, here we are. It says here the first step is to fair the curves in the hull. I have no idea . . . Yes, I have. What they want me to do first is take this chisel and from this block of wood form the hull. Here, Ussy, you take this book and read the instructions to me while I'm fairing out the curves in the hull."

Across from Mr. Suffrin, Ussy sat on the floor with the book in his hands. "It says here you should build a simple cradle and line it with something soft to hold the model while it's being worked on. What's a bowsprit?"

"I don't know. We'll have to look in the dictionary. But I think that comes a lot later, doesn't it?"

"I'm over here on page twenty-four. Hey, this is interesting. Over here on page forty-three they want you to bore fifty-four deadeyes and seize them and then you run reeves through them. What're reeves?"

"A reeve is a rope of onions," answered Mr. Suffrin. "But we don't need to worry about that now. We

154

don't even have the cradle for the hull built yet. A reeve is also an administrative official, like a ship's steward. Ouch. Nicked my finger that time."

"I just can't think," said Ussy, "why they'd want you to run a rope of onions or a ship's steward through your deadeyes. That sounds funny. Deadeyes are . . . look, I brought your dictionary in here. Here's what it says about deadeyes. A deadeye is a rounded, flattish wooden block encircled by rope or an iron band and pierced with holes to receive the lanyard used to set up shrouds and stays and for other purposes. Now I just don't know what they'd want you to run ropes of onions or officials through them for. I wonder what a lanyard is. This is certainly a terrible book of instructions. They didn't write it clear. Listen to this: Tops'l sheets should be set up with four C-4 blocks to spider rings at the foot of the mast-foreside and belay to the fife rail. Then you're supposed to move the lower double block forward to mizzenmast if it fouls the pinrail and then put some other rings in the cabin top. I think I'm going crazy, reading this stuff."

"We'll figure it all out when we get to it," said Mr. Suffrin. "Step by step. It'll probably take us the rest of the summer."

"It says over here that the clews should lead through the fairleader in top and set up or belay to pinrail P. and S. sheets belay to fife rails. You know what a Flemish horse is?"

"Ussy, don't read any more instructions."

"A Flemish horse is a short footrope. Why didn't they just say so?"

"Just let me live long enough," said Mr. Suffrin, wielding his chisel. "That's all I ask."

Ussy laid the book of instructions aside. He lay flat on the floor on his stomach gazing at Mr. Suffrin and after a while his thoughts, which had been lying scattered in his mind for days, began to amass. He put his legs in the air, joining his heels together, and began a confession that, to his own ears, sounded queer and not part of anything that concerned him. "Well," he said. "I'm tired. Like I've been sick but I haven't. I just figured out what's wrong with me. I haven't got any starch left in me, that's all. I've worked like a beast all summer and now it's almost over and I haven't got a thing to show for it except a few measly dollars."

Dignified and oddly childlike at the same time, Mr. Suffrin set the hull of his ship on the floor and, absorbed in it, ran a finger over its uneven, chiseled lines. His short, white curls, pink cheeks, and vividly blue eyes made Ussy think of Santa Claus. His socks were in wrinkles, pushed down over the tops of his shoes; his white shirt had a scorch mark on the collar. He was delighted with his new project and plainly just itching to get on with it but he transferred his attention from it to Ussy and said, "But that can't be true. You've lived all summer. Don't you think that counts for anything?"

"That Luke Wilder," said Ussy. "He messed up my plans."

"The dependent one," said Mr. Suffrin. "I

remember. What happened? You have to help him again?"

"Yes."

"And you didn't want to."

"It wasn't that I didn't want to," argued Ussy. "But zounds. It sure takes all the starch out of a guy. To work your guts out all summer for somebody else. Luke's okay; I got him to thinking a little bit different than he used to. But I keep thinking about his father. I think I almost hate him. He isn't good for anything that I can think of. But he's going to have his trial and I guess I'm going to have to go to it and stand up and be a witness for him. The other guys are all lying about what happened that day out at the Snyder farm."

"I think you'll make a good witness," commented Mr. Suffrin.

Ussy sat up and his breath began to quicken and his eyes began to flash. Emphatically he said, "I'm going to tell the judge exactly what happened. The whole truth and nothing but the truth. It makes me sick that the others can lie about it and people believe them."

"I was a witness at a trial one time," said Mr. Suffrin.

"He'll believe me," said Ussy. "The judge will. He's got to. Otherwise Mr. Wilder will go to prison."

"I think probably your argument will persuade the judge to the right decision," said Mr. Suffrin. His voice curved around his words as if the sound of them was pleasing.

"I'm going to tell the judge what William Make-

peace Thackeray said about dependence being a perpetual call upon humanity," said Ussy, standing up.
"That'll give him something to think about. Packy Snyder gives me a pain in my whatzis. He's got more than
Mr. Wilder will ever have and knows more than Mr.
Wilder will ever know but he treated that poor old
man worse than he would a stray dog. He ought to be
on trial, too. For not answering *his* call to humanity.
I think I'll tell the judge that."

"I think that's a splendid idea," said Mr. Suffrin.

"I think I'll tell him I answered my call to
humanity and I don't see why other people can't. No,
that sounds like bragging, doesn't it?"

"It might," said Mr. Suffrin.

Ussy stepped over Mr. Suffrin's tools and pieces
of his ship-building kit and began to hop around the
room, first on one foot and then on the other. His
starch was back. By golly, it was back! "I don't care,"
he said. "I don't care if it sounds like bragging. It's the
truth. I answered my call to humanity. I didn't want to
but I did."

"I know what you mean," said Mr. Suffrin. "I've
answered a few calls to humanity myself. You're right;
it sure takes the starch out of a guy."

"Luke told me he wanted to be like me," said
Ussy. "Isn't that the crackiest thing you ever heard?"

"It's a compliment," said Mr. Suffrin. "Probably
one of the nicest ones you'll ever receive."

Ussy started to laugh. "It's so funny. I keep getting the funniest ideas about him saying that. I keep
thinking what if he started doing everything I do.

What if I started taking two baths every day and Luke did, too. When I first met him he didn't look like he'd ever had a bath. Wouldn't it be funny if now he'd start taking two every day?"

"Let's work on the ship some more," suggested Mr. Suffrin and his voice was so practical but Ussy had turned to look at his teacher and in the vivid blue eyes he saw respect shining. For him, Ussy Mock. He stared at Mr. Suffrin and Mr. Suffrin stared back. "Well, zounds," whispered Ussy finally.

"Let's work on the ship some more," said Mr. Suffrin in an easy, offhand way. As if every day he gave his respect to one of his students. "Come on back and read some more of the plans to me while I work on the hull."

Ussy went back and sat down across from his teacher. He picked up the book of instructions for the ship model and opened it. He began to read at random. "Well, let's see now. On this page I'm looking at they talk about monkey rail stanchions. What're those, I wonder. Wait a minute. I'll look it up. I'd better look up mizzenmasts, too. And bollards. They talk about those, too."

"Zounds," said Mr. Suffrin.

"We'll be here till Christmas," said Ussy.

"I think so," agreed Mr. Suffrin. "Zounds."

❧ ABOUT THE AUTHORS

Vera and Bill Cleaver, whose insights into the wisdom and dignity of young people have proclaimed them among the best-loved writers of contemporary children's books, have been twice nominated for the distinguished National Book Award. They began their career in writing for young people with their unforgettable portrait of ELLEN GRAE, and continue to produce equally compelling stories and characters which have played a part in changing the course of children's literature today.

Vera Cleaver was born in South Dakota; Bill Cleaver in Seattle, Washington. They now pursue their writing as well as their special interests in art, music, and nature, from their home in Lutz, Florida.

160